THE MYSTERIOUS
MR. BADMAN

THE
MYSTERIOUS
MR. BADMAN

A YORKSHIRE BIBLIOMYSTERY

W. F. HARVEY

With an Introduction by
Martin Edwards

Poisoned Pen
PRESS

Published by Poisoned Pen Press, an imprint of Sourcebooks,
in association with the British Library
P.O. Box 4410, Naperville, Illinois 60567-4410
(630) 961-3900
sourcebooks.com

The Mysterious Mr. Badman was originally published in the
UK in 1934 by Pawling and Ness Ltd, London.

Cataloging-in-Publication Data is on file with the Library of Congress.

Printed and bound in the United States of America.
VP 10 9 8 7 6 5 4 3 2 1

Contents

Introduction

The Mysterious Mr. Badman is a long-forgotten but entertaining crime novel, its light-heartedness all the more unexpected given the author's reputation as a master of the macabre. The teasing tone is set right from the start, in the opening sentence: "When at two o'clock on a sultry July afternoon Athelstan Digby undertook to keep an eye on the contents of the old bookshop in Keldstone High Street, he deliberately forgot to mind his own business."

Digby is—at least, as far as I am aware—the only blanket manufacturer to feature as the protagonist of a crime novel. He is holidaying in Keldstone, where his nephew, Jim Pickering, contemplates taking over the local doctor's practice. Keldstone is in the Cleveland Hills in Yorkshire, which was the native county of the author, W. F. Harvey, and the pleasant setting contributes to the charm of the novel.

Digby offers to look after a bookshop owned by his landlord and is perplexed to find three different customers—a vicar, a chauffeur, and a stranger to the neighbourhood—all asking for a copy of John Bunyan's *The Life and Death of Mr. Badman*. As he says, with a mastery of understatement, "I can't help thinking that there is something at the back of it." Indeed there is, and the plot soon begins to thicken.

Everything I have learned about William Fryer Harvey (1885–1937) indicates that he was an admirable and indeed heroic individual who, over the years, experienced more than his fair share of misfortune. He was, at least, lucky to be born into an affluent family. The Harveys came from Leeds and were prominent members of the city's community of Quakers. One of seven children, he published a memoir of his early days, *We Were Seven*, in 1935. He was educated at Quaker Schools in York and in Reading before going up to Balliol College, Oxford, the alma mater of many crime writers as well as such fictional detectives of the Golden Age as Lord Peter Wimsey, Dr. Gideon Fell, and R. C. Woodthorpe's Nicholas Slade. Harvey took an M.A. in 1910 but illness disrupted his studies as well as his plans to qualify as a doctor.

Interesting biographical notes about Harvey are to be found in David Stuart Davies's introduction to a 2009 collection of Harvey's short stories, *The Beast with Five Fingers*. Davies explains that Harvey sought to aid his recovery by taking a voyage around the world, in the course of which he spent some time in Australia and New Zealand and argues that these experiences helped to fuel his imagination. He became interested in adult education, hoping to assist those less fortunate than himself. When war broke out, he joined the Friends' Ambulance Unit and spent time in Flanders. Subsequently, he qualified as a surgeon and became a surgeon-lieutenant in the Royal Navy. During that time occurred an incident which had profound consequences for him. He risked his life in order to carry out an amputation of a senior petty officer's arm after the man became trapped in the wrecked and flooded engine room of a destroyer which was about to break in two. As a result, the patient was rescued, but the escaping oil fumes caused serious damage to Harvey's lungs. He lost consciousness and had to be dragged out to save his own life. He was awarded the Albert Medal for gallantry at sea, but his health never recovered.

After the war, Harvey returned to the field of adult education, only for health problems to enforce his retirement in 1925. He and his wife, Margaret, moved to Switzerland in the hope that the clean air would assist his breathing, but they missed England and returned to live in Weybridge. He was able to devote time to writing, and the couple moved to Letchworth in 1935. At the time of his death, aged fifty-two, he was President of the Friends' Historical Society; shortly before he died, he was working on a paper about "the past training of members in the art of Quaker worship as shown in our literature from the seventeenth century to the early nineteenth."

Harvey's first published book, *Midnight House and Other Tales*, appeared in 1910. Ten years later it was followed by *The Misadventures of Athelstan Digby*, a collection of loosely linked stories. Two more collections of eerie stories appeared in his lifetime: *The Beast with Five Fingers* (1928) and *Moods and Tenses* (1933). Digby reappeared in *The Mysterious Mr. Badman*, published in 1934 by the small firm of Pawling and Ness. Unfortunately, Pawling and Ness ceased trading shortly thereafter, a development which seems rather typical of Harvey's bad luck. As a result, copies of this novel have until now been in very short supply.

There is an eerie quality to Harvey's best stories which is subtle and unpredictable. There is a touch of Poe and a dash of M. R. James, but his writing is distinctive. He trades in murder, mystery, and the supernatural, but occasional touches of humour lighten several otherwise disturbing tales. A splendid example, surprisingly little-known, is "The Habeas Corpus Club," a witty and original "bibliomystery." "August Heat" and "The Dabblers" are stories of considerable merit, but his most famous work is undoubtedly "The Beast with Five Fingers," which concerns a disembodied hand. The story was filmed in 1946, with a screenplay by Curt Siodmak and a score by Max Steiner. Peter Lorre gives an especially memorable performance. Another version of the story appeared in a segment within the mid-sixties horror anthology film, *Dr. Terror's House of Horrors*, starring Peter Cushing and Christopher Lee. The success of the earlier film seems to have sparked a revival of interest in Harvey's work. A posthumous collection of stories, *The Arm of Mrs. Egan and Other Stories*, appeared in 1951. These stories, which Harvey had left in manuscript, included a tantalising and first-rate crime story, "The Lake." He will no doubt always be regarded primarily as a horror writer, but as this book shows, his contribution to the crime genre is worth remembering.

Martin Edwards
www.martinedwardsbooks.com

A Note from the Publisher

The original novels and short stories reprinted in the British Library Crime Classics series were written and published in a period ranging, for the most part, from the 1890s to the 1960s. There are many elements of these stories which continue to entertain modern readers; however, in some cases there are also uses of language, instances of stereotyping, and some attitudes expressed by narrators or characters which may not be endorsed by the publishing standards of today. We acknowledge therefore that some elements in the works selected for reprinting may continue to make uncomfortable reading for some of our audience. With this series, British Library Publishing and Poisoned Pen Press aim to offer a new readership a chance to read some of the rare books of the British Library's collections in an affordable paperback format, to enjoy their merits, and to look back into the world of the twentieth century as portrayed by its writers. It is not possible to separate these stories from the history of their writing and as such the following stories are presented as they were originally published with the inclusion of minor edits made for consistency of style and sense, and with pejorative terms of an extremely offensive nature partly obscured. We welcome feedback from our readers.

I
Three Men Call by Day

When at two o'clock on a sultry July afternoon Athelstan Digby undertook to keep an eye on the contents of the old bookshop in Keldstone High Street, he deliberately forgot to mind his own business.

He was a blanket manufacturer by trade. He had come to Keldstone partly for a holiday—he had long wished to explore these villages in the Cleveland Hills—and partly to advise his nephew, Jim Pickering, who was thinking of taking over Dr. Jacobs's practice after acting for some months as the old man's locum tenens.

Jim had found for him these comfortable lodgings at Daniel Lavender's. He had a bedroom above the shop and a little sitting-room at the back that looked out over the disused graveyard of the parish church northwards to the moors. It was because he felt completely at home in his surroundings and had a real liking for his stout little landlord and that tall, gaunt Mrs. Lavender, who was so good a baker of bread and cakes and scones, that he had volunteered to take charge of the shop, so that both could attend the funeral of Dan's cousin in Mardale.

At first they would not hear of it; but, once convinced that he was in earnest, the old couple proceeded to take down the last shutters of their reserve. Mr. Lavender showed him where he kept the priced catalogue that could be consulted when the figures pencilled inside a volume were indecipherable; he explained what to do with the sixpenny boxes, if it came on to rain. Mrs. Lavender entrusted him with the key of the larder and gave minute instructions about warming the teapot before he made his cup of tea.

"I'll put it all out ready for you," she said, "but in case you fancy anything extra, you'll know where to get it for yourself."

Mr. and Mrs. Lavender set off a little after two. From his comfortable arm-chair in the shop, Athelstan Digby watched them go down the High Street arm in arm, like two oddly assorted volumes from the shelves, Daniel Lavender, leather bound, fat and stumpy; Mrs. Lavender, cloth bound, tall and thin.

For an hour he read undisturbed. The High Street seemed asleep; the only sounds that broke the quiet of the afternoon came from the station, where they were shunting trucks. Then the church clock chimed three, the shop-bell rang, and his first customer entered, an old lady who had picked out a volume from the sixpenny box. Ten minutes later a schoolboy was asking what books they had on wireless. They had no books on wireless, Mr. Digby discovered; but the boy seemed satisfied with the purchase of *Rabbit Breeding for Profit.*

The takings of the till amounted to one and twopence, when once again the bell tinkled and a clergyman stepped into the shop. He was stout and elderly, shaven, but not clean shaven. He nodded at Mr. Digby.

"I just want to have a look round," he said, and began fingering the books. The fingers were stained brown with nicotine; the creases at the back of his neck were thick and fat. "An unpleasant-looking customer," thought Mr. Digby. "I expect he's on the prowl for sermons and doesn't want to be disturbed."

"Can't I assist you, sir?" he said at last. "Mr. Lavender is out, and I have volunteered to look after the shop in his absence."

The clergyman looked up with a start.

"I was seeing if you had a book," he said, "which was recommended to me the other day and which I must confess I have never read—Bunyan's *Life and Death of Mr. Badman*."

"I'll turn up the catalogue," Mr. Digby replied. "If it is on the shelves, it should be somewhere over in that corner. I'll get the steps, and you can look round for yourself."

Mr. Lavender's catalogue was arranged on a system difficult to decipher, but Mr. Digby at last discovered that, though Bunyan was represented by two copies of *Pilgrim's Progress* and one of the *Holy War*, no mention was made of *Mr. Badman*. He looked up to find the clergyman standing on the steps, busy examining the yellow-backed French novels on the top shelf.

"Entertaining but unprofitable reading," said that gentleman, with a leer, "and very discreetly housed by our friend Lavender. Well, well! If *Mr. Badman* can't be found, I must be off; but if by any chance Mr. Lavender does come across a copy, I wish he would keep it for me and drop me a line. The Reverend Percival Offord, Worpleswick Vicarage. You might tell him, too, that if he could let me have a copy in the next day or two, I should be especially grateful. A charming old fellow, Lavender! Good afternoon!"

Athelstan Digby felt the air of the shop less musty when Mr. Offord had gone.

"I hope Lavender will find a copy of the book for him," he thought. "It should prove congenial reading."

Two more customers, and then soon after four a man came in and asked if he could look round for a bit of reading.

"What sort of book do you want?" said Mr. Digby.

"Oh, anything; I'm not particular, but I do like a bit of reading in the evening. I'll just see what you've got myself."

Mr. Digby watched him—a little man, sandy-haired, quick-fingered, silent of tread. He tried to place him. Solicitor's clerk? No, he was too shifty-looking for that. He would not impress confidence in clients. Under-manager of a multiple shop? Possibly, but obviously not a successful under-manager. The Reverend Percival Offord reminded him of a sleek ferret; this man had more of the lean fox about him.

"By the way," he said at last, "you don't happen to have a book called *The Life and Death of Mr. Badman*? My wife was talking about it the other day. She said it was by Bunyan, and I said there was no such book and that she'd got mixed up with the title and author. I told her that very likely there was a *Life and Death of Bunyan* by a Mr. Badman. I knew a Doctor Badman when I was a lad, but it's not a common name."

"Your wife was right," said Mr. Digby, "but I happen to know that we haven't got the book in stock. You see..."

Mr. Fox pricked up his ears and turned his head to the speaker.

"After all," thought Mr. Digby, "it's none of his business who called this afternoon." "You see," he went on, "I chanced to turn up Bunyan in the catalogue an hour ago: two copies of *Pilgrim's Progress* and the *Holy War*. If *Mr. Badman* had been there, I should have been sure to notice it."

"It might be on the shelves and not in the catalogue," said the other. "But no doubt you're right, and I'll have to give my wife best. All the same it's a funny title for a book."

"You're hard to convince," said Mr. Digby. "But there's the Encyclopaedia. Look up Bunyan and see for yourself."

The man went off, seemingly satisfied, but without making a purchase.

As he drank his tea in Mrs. Lavender's kitchen, keeping one eye on the shop door, Mr. Digby found himself wondering if there was anything beyond coincidence that would account for two men in one short afternoon asking for the same book. If the book had been more common, he would have been less surprised; but it was a queer volume to be in demand, and the two men who demanded it struck him as being queer too. "Queer customers" was just the appropriate phrase to describe them. He had, however, even more unusual things to think about—the peculiar excellence of Mrs. Lavender's bilberry jam and the light-heartedness of her home-made cakes.

After tea he sold a fine copy of Duck's *Thresher* to a man who evidently knew something about books, and *Browning for Beginners* to a girl who looked as if she might be a governess.

Then just after half-past five a chauffeur came in. He wasted no time in beating about the bush. Had they a copy of the *Life and Death of Mr. Badman*? He had got the name written on a slip of paper, in case he should forget it, and he handed the slip of paper to Mr. Digby.

"I'm sorry we haven't," he said. "There's *Pilgrim's Progress* and the *Holy War*; the latter is quite a good copy."

"The Holy War be blowed!" said the chauffeur, with a grin. "I had four and a half years of it and I didn't see much holiness, I can tell you. But I've got to be at Scarborough by seven. If you've not got the book, that's all I want to know"; and he was out of the shop before Mr. Digby could reply. He recognised, however, the tune that the chauffeur was whistling. "Yes, we have no bananas," appeared to him as highly appropriate.

Mr. Digby took up the slip of paper and looked at it carefully. It seemed to be a leaf torn from a note-book. The name of the book and author was written in pencil in large printed characters.

It was all very curious. Three men in a little over three hours had asked for the same book. What, again, was the connection? The ferret and the fox were beasts of ill omen, but there was nothing wrong with the chauffeur. He was as honest as daylight.

Half an hour passed and then again the shop-bell rang. The customer this time was a small boy, who carried a heavy parcel.

"I've got some books to sell," he said, "second-hand. What'll you give me for the lot?"

"Bring them over to the desk here, sonny, and let's have a look at them.—Hall and Knight's *Algebra*, Locke's *Arithmetic*, *A Peep Behind the Scenes*, *Common Objects of the Seashore*;—not much good, I'm afraid;—*Freshwater Molluscs*, with Plates;—that might be worth a little; and—great Caesar! *The Life and Death of Mr. Badman*! Where did you get these books from?"

"Miss Conyers of Deepdale End, she gave them to me this morning. She said as how they were no use to her and that Mr. Lavender would very likely give me something for them. I've got some more at home, but they were too heavy to bring all at once."

"And what might your name be, sonny?"

"Samuel Albert Johnson. My father's gardener up at Deepdale End."

Mr. Digby turned over the books.

"I'll give you seven shillings for the lot," he said, "or shall we say eight shillings?" After all, there was something owing to the name.

"Right you are," said the boy, his sparkling eyes betraying the nonchalance of his voice, "and I'll take sixpennorth of it in coppers."

Mr. Digby produced the money from his pocket. It was probably more than the books were worth, but this was his show, his very own adventure. It was closing time too. He went out into the street and brought in the shilling and six-penny boxes. There was thunder in the air and not a breath of wind. The Lavenders would be lucky if they got back dry-shod. He locked the door of the shop—Daniel Lavender would put up the shutters—and went into the kitchen with his book. It was a thin volume, neatly bound in calf. As a book there was nothing peculiar to note about it. There was no inscription on the fly-leaf. Was it this particular volume, he wondered, that was the object of the afternoon's inquiries? Would his queer customers have been satisfied with any copy?

When an hour later he gave an account of his stewardship to Mr. Lavender, he had many questions to ask the bookseller.

"In the first place," said Mr. Digby, "whose is the book, yours or mine? I paid for it, of course; but, strictly speaking, I was acting as your agent, though we had made no mention of purchasing books. However, there seems to be a demand for this volume, and it may be a profitable investment."

"There's nothing special about it," said Lavender, turning the pages. "It's in good condition; that's about all you can say. You are welcome to keep it, anyhow. It beats me what they wanted it for."

"And who exactly are they? The Reverend Percival Offord, to begin with?"

"He is the vicar of Worpleswick. Not exactly popular. Drinks a bit more than is good for him and his parish. He's a great hand at chess. I've nothing against him, but he isn't interested in books."

"And number two—the foxy fellow? He had a face something like this." Mr. Digby took a pencil from his pocket and began to draw.

"No I can't place him. He's not a Keldstone man."

"And the chauffeur?"

Again Mr. Lavender was at fault. Samuel Albert Johnson,

however, he did know, or rather his father; and he saw no reason to doubt the boy's story of how the book came into his possession.

"Well, it's all very queer," said Mr. Digby at last. "It may, of course, be a coincidence; but I can't help thinking that there is something at the back of it. In the meantime I think it would be best to say nothing about the matter. We will wait and see if anything happens."

Daniel Lavender promised silence.

Mr. Digby got up from his chair and through the open window looked out on to the deserted High Street.

"Any sign of Mr. Badman?" asked Daniel Lavender, with a laugh.

"I was wondering what had become of that thunder-storm," Mr. Digby replied. "It's intolerably close. Anyhow, I see you have some useful shutters to the shop, in case Mr. Badman does chance to call."

II
One Man Calls by Night

IT WAS INDEED INSUFFERABLY HOT, A NIGHT SUCH AS
no conscientious blanket-maker, whose trade-mark was a
golden fleece, could be expected to appreciate. Long after
his usual hour for retirement, Mr. Digby sat in his little back
sitting-room overlooking the churchyard, reading. His book
was a volume of reminiscences of a former vicar of Keldstone,
who had more than a local reputation as an antiquary. Before
him on the table was spread a large scale ordnance map. Truly
the district was a fascinating one, with its series of deep valleys
running up into the heart of the moors, each with its beck,
half stream, half river, fringed in springtime, Mr. Lavender
told him, by miles of short-stemmed, blue-leaved daffodils.
And the names of the outlying farms, Outershaw, Hangman's
Slack, Muggerswipe, Black Easter. Already he had planned
half a dozen walks which would put Jim on his mettle. His
nephew should carry the rucksack and do the uphill talking;
that was all the handicap that Mr. Digby asked.

The church clock struck eleven; he put out the lamp

and crossed the landing to his bedroom. The process of undressing was with Mr. Digby an elaborate but unhurried ritual. He respected his long-suffering clothes. From his right-hand breast pocket he drew a bulky leather wallet, the typed minutes of the last Board Meeting of the British and Colonial Bible Society, a prospectus of the Central Sumatra Consolidated Rubber Company, and a cutting from the *Times* of a recent sale at Christie's, where some of the works of his favourite Dutch Masters had changed hands at lamentably low figures. The contents of his right-hand pocket he arranged in a row on the dressing-table; the contents of his thirteen other pockets he methodically disposed of in a similar manner. A leather purse, a bunch of keys, three of which belonged to forgotten locks, a large knife, containing an implement for removing stones from horses' hoofs (needless to say, Mr. Digby had never removed a stone from a horse's hoof), a bundle of string, and his trousers were disposed of. From his waistcoat came his watch and chain, a pair of surgical scissors, a fountain-pen, a flat round circular pincushion, an ivory paper-knife, three elastic bands, and ten foreign stamps, neatly torn from the corners of their envelopes, which he was keeping for the first boy he should meet who was interested in stamps. From his ticket pocket came three unsurrendered railway tickets. He had had them for over a year, but some boys collected tickets as well as stamps. A pocket compass, a silver fruit-knife, and a folding lens completed the bill of lading. The three last items were in constant use when Athelstan Digby took a holiday. He liked to study the lie of the land; he enjoyed eating a ripe apple; and he was a more than competent field botanist.

Mr. Digby half closed the window—he believed that a little fresh air went a very long way—placed his boots outside the door, said his prayers, and got into bed. It was a feather bed, and, though he usually preferred them to the most hygienic of spring mattresses, on this particular July night he longed for something hard and cool from which he could hold himself aloof. He thought of his nephew and the boy's prospects. There seemed a good deal to be said for his settling in Keldstone. He had always liked a country life; the cottage hospital was unusually well equipped and would give him an opportunity for the surgical work for which he had a natural bent. Dr. Jacobs's practice was unopposed and, in the hands of a young and energetic successor, could easily be extended. There were some interesting people living in the district, Mr. Stillwinter, for example. Jim might well go farther and fare worse. The boy, of course, should marry—all doctors should marry—and then perhaps one of the sons, not necessarily the eldest, would take his place in the old firm of Digby, Dyson, and Coppleston. If Mrs. Jim turned out to be a sensible girl, he would leave his pictures to his nephew. His Bradborough friends, of course, expected that his collection would be eventually housed in the corporation gallery.

That bright young man from Oxford, who had recently been appointed curator and who had written that impossible little brochure on Cezanne, had always by his gracious condescension conveyed to Mr. Digby the impression that such an action was expected of him. There was something rather attractive, certainly, in the idea of a Digby Bequest. Perhaps it would be better to wait and see.

Mr. Digby tossed on his feather bed. The night was very oppressive, and sleep was slow in coming. He began to count sheep going through a gate, and then his thoughts ran off after them to the prices at the latest wool sales, and then back to blankets. It was horribly hot. Then he tried to recall his summer holidays. Back, back he went in time, until at last at High Force in Middleton-in-Teesdale in 1885 sleep overtook him.

He woke up to find the moonlight streaming into the room. Could he be bothered to get up and draw the curtains? Sleepily, he looked at his watch, a quarter to two. And then his ear caught a faint sound that came from somewhere outside his room, a rustling sound, and then a creak. Mice perhaps in the sitting-room, scuttling about in the paper that blocked the empty grate. Old boards creak, old furniture creaks, he told himself (old joints, too, Mr. Digby), especially in weather like this. But what really was it? He listened again more carefully. The noise hardly seemed to come from the sitting-room. Mr. Digby was now thoroughly awake. Slipping on a pair of slippers, he opened the door and stepped out into the passage. It was carpeted and he tiptoed silently towards the stairs, passing Mr. and Mrs. Lavender's room on the right. Again he listened. There was the ticking of the kitchen clock; there was the sound of Daniel Lavender's snore; but there was something else, a rustle and a footfall, that seemed to come from the shop beneath. He wondered if burglars had indeed entered the house, and for a moment thought of arousing his landlord. But Daniel was a heavy sleeper. His knock on the door would only give the alarm to the intruder, if intruder there was; and if intruder there was not, he would only make himself ridiculous. He would go down into the shop and see for himself.

Silently, slowly he groped his way downstairs. The house that Daniel Lavender occupied was old and rambling. On the ground floor it was divided by a corridor that ran the length of the building. At the foot of the stairs a door to the right gave access to the glass-partitioned office which, in turn, opened into the shop. At the other end of the shop a second door opened into the corridor immediately opposite the door of the back parlour, which in turn communicated with the kitchen and a little paved yard that abutted on to the old graveyard of the parish church.

Mr. Digby entered the shop through the office. The room was completely dark, the shutters screening the moonlight. But a screen more effectual than darkness was afforded by the arrangement of the tall cases, which divided the floor space into recesses, where someone even now might be lurking. Mr. Digby strained every nerve to listen. And then he heard quite distinctly the sound of a door opening. It was not the door at the farther end of the shop. The sound was too distant for that. It seemed rather to come from the other side of the corridor, from the back parlour. Mr. Digby saw at once what had happened. If burglar there was, he had left the shop by one door at the same time that Mr. Digby had entered it by the other and was now probably making his way through the kitchen to the yard at the back. He retraced his steps into the corridor and followed him. He had no matches, and his progress was slow. But the back parlour was not wholly dark, and the kitchen beyond was light enough to see that it was empty. But the larder window was open and beneath it was a broken saucer of milk.

"An emergency exit," thought Mr. Digby. Obviously this was no cat burglar. What was he to do now? He fastened the window, found candles and matches, and made a careful inspection of the ground-floor rooms. As far as he could see, they showed no signs of disturbance. In any case it would be useless at that hour to arouse the Lavenders. Mr. Badman had been and gone; but who Mr. Badman was and what Mr. Badman wanted were problems that would await the morning.

Mr. Digby slept late. The adventure of the night had given him an excellent appetite for breakfast, and, the meal finished, he made his way down to the shop, where he found Mr. Lavender busy with his catalogues in the little office.

The bookseller listened with interest to Mr. Digby's story. Obviously, the first thing to do was to see if anything were missing. The small amount of cash which Mr. Lavender kept in a locked drawer of his desk was as small as it had been on the previous evening, but no smaller. The books did not seem to be disarranged, but it would have been an easy matter to remove volumes from the shelves without detection. There were no footprints. But in the kitchen they found Mrs. Lavender lamenting over a broken saucer, and Polly, the servant girl, with a face flushed with indignant denial.

"Don't say anything to the old lady," Mr. Lavender said, as he took Mr. Digby aside. "She'd be scared to death at the idea of burglars. We'll talk the matter over in your room, where we shan't be interrupted."

"To begin with," said Mr. Digby, "was there a burglar, or was I alarmed only by a concatenation of suggestive noises?"

"Then what about the broken saucer? I heard Mrs. Lavender tell the girl that she put the milk out for the kitten last thing before she went to bed. Besides, I don't think you're the sort of man, Mr. Digby, who would imagine things. No, I think we can take it that someone entered the house last night, and I think it's more than a coincidence that it should follow immediately after that curious business of yesterday afternoon."

"You mean that one of those three wanted to get hold of that book?"

"It looks like it on the face of things, don't it? At the same time I don't want to put the police on to the job. Mrs. Lavender is subject to palpitations, for one thing. For another, there's a lot of gossip in a little place like Keldstone, Mr. Digby, and gossip isn't good for trade."

"And yet on the other hand," said Mr. Digby, "if one of those three men is so anxious to secure my copy of *The Life and Death of Mr. Badman,* that he does not scruple to burgle your house, it looks as if I had got hold of a rather embarrassing possession and you of an equally embarrassing lodger."

Mr. Lavender received this statement with a silence that implied consent.

"I have it!" said Mr. Digby at last. "We will hoist these gentlemen with their own petard and at the same time rid ourselves of their unwelcome attentions."

He took a pen and a sheet of paper and began to write.

"Now," he said at last, "I think that notice, suitably displayed in one of your windows, should do the trick."

Mr. Lavender read it in some perplexity.

"WILL THE GENTLEMAN WHO TOOK BY MISTAKE
A COPY OF BUNYAN'S 'LIFE AND DEATH OF MR.
BADMAN,' RETURN IT AS SOON AS POSSIBLE, AS
THE BOOK IS IN DEMAND."

"I don't quite see what you are driving at," he said, as he scratched his head.

"It's quite simple," Mr. Digby answered. "Three people want that book. They read that notice and learn that it is not here. They learn, too, that someone else has walked off with it, and each will suspect the other. If there is to be any more burglary, it will not be your house that will suffer. All I have done is to set a thief to catch a thief."

"Mr. Digby, sir, you should have been a detective," cried Mr. Lavender, delightedly; and he hurried down into the shop to fix the notice.

III
Gaunt Lodge

Mr. Digby's plans for the morning were already made. He had received from Mr. Stillwinter, of Gaunt Lodge, an invitation to lunch. Jim Pickering was to join him there in the afternoon, when there was to be tennis for the young people. Digby and Stillwinter were little more than acquaintances. They had met five years before in Egypt, where they had shared the same table at a hotel, two cheerful old bachelors, leagued together in defence of their prejudices.

Philip Stillwinter had been a great traveller. He had spent long and lonely years in Arabia, Persia, and Thibet—he was an acknowledged authority on the flora of the last-named country—and would probably have been wandering still, had not a fractured thigh made him incapable of mounting a horse. So he had returned to Gaunt Lodge, Miss Stillwinter, his library, and his garden.

Mr. Digby enjoyed his four-mile walk up the wooded valley of Brock Beck, past the stone quarries on to Cadley Common, where the gypsies camped and from the northern edge of which he looked down upon Gaunt Lodge and its walled meadows, lying like a green handkerchief pinned out on the moor to dry in the July sun. The gentle monotonous whirr of the machine mower came up to him from below. The hay harvest had already begun. His host must have seen him standing against the sky-line, for, as Mr. Digby scrambled down the bracken-covered slope, following one of the narrow sheep tracks, he recognised the thin wiry figure of Stillwinter coming to meet him. They greeted each other warmly.

"Well, here you see me, anchored in my backwater," said Stillwinter. "'A passage perilous maketh a port pleasant'— you know the old adage. But the trouble is that so few ships put into this harbour. I'm a derelict, I suppose, and frighten them away. Green seaweed and barnacles! All the same, I've no right to complain. Olaf Wake's staying with me now. You've heard of him, of course? The economist. I used to know his mother well. He's a live wire, if there ever was one, though I distrust his politics. At the present moment I can't make up my mind if he keeps one young or only makes one feel very old. But come and have a look at my new rock garden before lunch."

He led the way to a corner of the garden, where two men with crow-bars were busy adjusting a huge boulder.

"It's fascinating work," Stillwinter explained, "and not nearly as simple as you might think. You must get the right angle, which is the natural angle, and no other. Lower your end a little, Brown, and bring that corner forward. Happily we haven't far to go for our stone. My sister says I'm turning the place into a veritable graveyard, but wait until next spring. She'll change her mind when she sees the gentians in June."

There were four at lunch. Mr. Digby sat on the right of Miss Stillwinter, a little birdlike creature, who hopped about from one topic of conversation to another, pecking shyly for crumbs of information. Opposite him was Mr. Olaf Wake. He was a man of middle height, dressed in a suit of Irish homespun. A little loud, Mr. Digby thought it was. His nose was long, his chin receding, and the eyes behind the rimless glasses were a light blue. Mr. Olaf Wake's tie and stockings were also blue and of a similar shade; but Mr. Digby attributed this to coincidence. It was inconceivable to him that a well-known economist could waste his time on anything so trivial as a colour scheme. There was no doubt that the man was very wide awake.

There were one or two points in connection with the heavy woollen industry on which he asked for information, and his questions showed that he was already exceedingly well informed. The conversation passed to the reconstruction of the devastated areas of northern France and the stabilisation of the franc; then to the stained glass in the cathedral of Chartres; the best way to preserve truffles; and the last recorded occasion on which the wild boar was hunted in England.

Mr. Wake spoke with ease and authority on everything that came his way. He monopolised the talk without his hearers being conscious of the evils of monopoly. Again and again Mr. Digby had to change his impression of a conceited young puppy that he would like to kick into that of an able young dog that he would willingly follow.

After lunch Wake withdrew to the library—there was an unfinished article that he had to get off by the afternoon post—and Stillwinter and Digby retired to the verandah.

"What do you think of young England, or rather young Ireland? He's more than half Irish, you know, and is unnecessarily proud of the fact."

"A remarkable young man," said Mr. Digby; "but is he never wrong?"

"That is the trouble with him," Stillwinter answered. "He's one of those all-round people that elude your grasp. You can never catch them out. Why, the other day, my gardener, who is the most unsuccessful backer of horses I have ever met, netted five pounds on a double. Wake had given him the tip. It seems he makes a point of studying horses' form. And now the man will eat out of his hand. Then there's the cook, one of the most independent old parties I have ever come across; he has shown her a new way of making sago puddings, and to-morrow, I believe, he is to give a demonstration in bottling loganberries. The cook, I might add, is as deaf as a door-post and is impervious to new ideas. Personal magnetism, I suppose. I only wish I'd got it."

"You've got a sound constitution at any rate," said Mr. Digby, "which at our age is all that we've a right to ask."

"Oh, I'm hard enough, if it comes to that. I've been sleeping out for the last six weeks. And none of your camp bedsteads for me, Digby! Give me a good ground sheet and a sleeping-bag and I'm happy. I've half a dozen sleeping-bags in the house now to choose from. Bought them in all sorts of outlandish spots, you know. Only last night I was trying to persuade Wake to try his hand at sleeping out, but the young beggar put me off. He reeled off some scientific stuff about relative humidity. Humidity, not humility. I'm left to inherit the earth, while Mr. Olaf reclines at ease on a goose feather bed, with the sheets turned down so bravely oh!"

Mr. Digby enjoyed his forty winks in the hot July sunshine. He was rather sorry when the young people came for tennis and the chairs were moved to the terrace above the lawn. There were the two daughters of the vicar, tall strapping wenches, who followed the otter hounds and smoked perpetually in between sets; Miss Conyers, a tall, graceful girl, who did not play as well as he hoped, especially when she was partnered by Jim; young Kynaston, just down from Oxford; and Olaf Wake. Wake, of course, was the best of the bunch. He had a deadly swerve, the secret of which he explained to Jim, who did not seem interested. Perhaps it was because he was still sleepy, perhaps it was because there was thunder in the air, but it seemed to Mr. Digby, as he sat in the shade under the mulberry tree, that the young people were rather at sixes and sevens. Was it because they were playing in the shadow of three old fogies, the Stillwinters and himself? But obviously the two Miss Drurys were rivals for the attention of young Kynaston. Jim, the easy going, for some reason did not seem to hit it off with Miss Conyers, and Wake, in his attempts to set everyone at ease, only succeeded in becoming an intolerable bore.

"Who the dickens is the little bounder?" asked Jim as they motored back to Keldstone. "An economist and fellow of his college? But what right does that give him to lay down the law on cancer research? It's a wonder to me how poor old Stillwinter can put up with him. Did you see him instructing Miss Conyers in the way to hold her racquet?"

"I did; and personally I thought she could gain by instruction."

Mr. Digby watched the dark, handsome face of his nephew flush with anger.

"With all due apologies, Uncle, you know very little about the game. Miss Conyers may not be a very brilliant player, but she can knock spots off those cup-hunting Drury girls whenever she wants to. She didn't to-day, I admit; but I don't blame her. It was too hot to take tennis seriously, and I've not got the right temperament to be her partner. That's all there is to it."

The car drew up outside Daniel Lavender's.

"You're coming in, of course?" said Mr. Digby. "I ordered supper for half-past seven, and I want to show you my latest purchase."

"A picture?"

"No, a book. And what is more, there is rather a curious story about the way it came into my possession. You are fond of solving mysteries. I can present you with a thoroughly intriguing one."

In the little upstairs sitting-room Mr. Digby recounted to his nephew the events of the preceding day.

"There is the book," he said, taking it down from the shelf. "There seems nothing peculiar about it to me. Let's see what your trained senses can make of it."

Jim picked up the volume and turned over the pages.

"Binding fairly new," he said, "no inscription on the fly-leaf, no price mark, dried eucalyptus leaf, used probably as a book-mark, at page thirty-four."

"Hullo!" said Mr. Digby, "I didn't notice that."

"May as well read those two pages," said Jim, "in case they contain a clue. It's buried treasure, perhaps. Eucalyptus—gum trees—Australia—bush-rangers—Mr. Badman. Nothing doing there, I'm afraid," he went on after a pause. "All the same it's rather an interesting prelude to adventure. Three men with but a single thought and one a shady looking parson. Suggestion number one: A cypher, of which this book contains the key. You remember Gabordiau's *Monsieur Le Coq*? Suggestion number two: A wager in the bar parlour of the 'Golden Crown.' Lavender vouches for the fact that our Worpleswick friend is not over-abstemious, you will remember. I can picture the scene: 'John Bunyan, the man who wrote *Pilgrim's Progress*. Ought to have tried his hand at a novel.' 'Well, what about *Mr. Badman*?' 'That was Fielding.' 'Fielding be blowed. John Bunyan wrote *The Life and Death of Mr. Badman*. I'll lay you a quid to a bob that Daniel Lavender has got a copy of the book on his shelves.'"

"Then why didn't they all come in together and see for themselves?" asked Mr. Digby.

"Offord wasn't a party to the bet. They sent him first as an impartial observer, he being in holy orders. He returns to say that the book is not there. The layer of the wager suggests that possibly his vision is defective. It is after four o'clock."

"When the pubs are shut," chuckled Mr. Digby. "How do you get over that?"

"Ask the landlord of the 'Golden Crown.' Private room it will have to be, not private bar. Emissary number two is dispatched, our friend Foxy. Foxy returns empty-handed but reports that the old gentleman in charge doesn't seem to know his job. Our wagerer writes the name of the book on a slip of paper, prints it, as he hears the gentleman is old."

"Steady on with the age," laughed Mr. Digby.

"Prints it," continued Jim, "and buttonholes a chauffeur who is carrying on a mild flirtation with Molly Ellaby, the barmaid. The chauffeur makes his report, and there the matter rests. To account for Samuel Johnson's visit one must invoke the long arm of coincidence. Your intruder by night is the original layer of the wager, whom you interrupt just as he is about to plant his own copy of *Mr. Badman* in an inaccessible shelf, where he would discover it by chance in the morning. How does that strike you for a plausible theory?"

"I think it almost too ingenious to be true," said Mr. Digby, "but it certainly has its points. Have you any more suggestions from that fertile brain of yours?"

"It might be worth while," said Jim, after a pause, "to ask Miss Conyers what she knows about the book. After all, it was she who gave it to the boy."

"I think I will," Mr. Digby answered. "She is a charming young lady. But why not ask her yourself? You are more likely to meet her than I am."

"Oh no! We don't often come across each other," said Jim, as he rose to leave, "and when we do, we are usually at cross purposes. But you are wrong about her tennis. When she's properly partnered, she's a first-class player."

IV

Two from Three
Leaves One

THAT NIGHT THE RAIN CAME. IT WAS THE WOLDS TO the east that caught the full force of the storm, but sufficient rain fell in Keldstone to lay the dust of weeks. Mr. Digby, shaving by the open window, decided that pre-eminently it was a day for a walk. Impatiently he glanced through his correspondence as he did justice to Mrs. Lavender's ham and eggs. Letters would have to wait. Letters on a holiday were a mistake. Appeals for subscriptions were almost a crime. But of course those children in Back Bannister Street ought to get some sort of a seaside outing. If he disliked Canon Godfrey, it was no reason why they should suffer, and he wrote out a cheque for the enclosed stamped envelope before he exchanged his slippers for his boots.

He put his map in his pocket, borrowed an empty cocoa tin from Mrs. Lavender for any rare flowers that he might find, and filled it in the meantime with half a pound of raisins which he bought at the grocer's opposite. The bulges in the figure of the old bachelor were a matter of no concern to him. They only served as a reminder that he was on holiday.

He went in the direction of Gaunt Lodge, but followed a different path from the one he had taken the preceding day. On the fringe of a beech wood above Brock Beck he made his first discovery of importance. The cocoa tin was emptied of its raisins and two spikes of the bee orchis took their place.

"Rather early in the morning to start eating raisins," thought Mr. Digby; so he took the minutes of the British and Colonial Bible Society from their envelope and made up a neat paper package, which he fastened with one of the three elastic bands from his waistcoat pocket. Then, with the satisfaction of feeling that he had shown himself prepared for all emergencies, he resumed his way.

At Kildale Mill he stopped to watch the peat-brown water swirling over the ruined weir, and then struck up on to the moor, choosing a patch that had been burned two years ago and which was now carpeted with green bilberry and bell heather. The walking was easy and he made good progress. It was extraordinarily peaceful. The only sound came from a lark, lost in the blue. There was no one in sight, no one, that is, except the young lady who stood silhouetted against the sky-line, apparently lost in admiration of the view. Then, as he looked, she turned and began to walk quickly towards him. It was Miss Conyers, a deeply agitated Miss Conyers, very different from the reserved, slightly cynical young lady he had met the preceding afternoon.

"Oh, Mr. Digby," she said, "something awful has happened behind the peat stacks over there. A man has shot himself. Please come at once and see if there is anything you can do."

"Bless my soul!" said Mr. Digby. "Is he…is he dead?"

"His eyes were wide open. There was a revolver and an awful wound in his head."

"Come and show me the place," he said, "and tell me all about it."

"There's nothing to tell. I left home an hour ago for a walk, meaning to cross over by the peat stacks to the Countersett Road. I never noticed him until I was almost on top of him. He was almost hidden by the peat."

"I am afraid it must have shaken you up pretty badly. Sit down here, my dear lady, and rest. You will be within call, if I need your help. These things are bound to be agitating. I am afraid I do not carry brandy, but if these raisins…"

Miss Conyers laughed.

"I shall be all right in a minute," she said. "I am a bit upset, as you can see; but if you wouldn't mind going on alone, I'll wait here as you suggest."

Mr. Digby found the place without difficulty. Some farmer with rights of turbary had been busy with his stock of winter fuel. A score or more of peat stacks some five feet high stood in a rough circle. As he approached, a black-faced ewe with her lamb scuttled off from the shelter of the nearest. A minute later he was face to face with the body. It lay propped up against the peat, the head bent forward. Mr. Digby knelt down and touched the cold hand, the hand that did not hold the pistol. Then he looked into the face, marred by a horrible wound above the temple, and recognised to his utter amazement the second seeker after *Mr. Badman*, Foxy, the sandy-haired and stealthy-footed.

Mr. Digby rose to his feet and wiped the perspiration

from his brow. What in the world could it all mean? How did this man come to be lying dead on the moor? And how long had he been there? Was it murder or suicide? Of course he would have to report to the police, but, as he was practically the first person on the spot, it might be as well to jot down what he had found.

He took out his pocket compass and began to make notes on the back of an envelope. Time, 10.30 a.m. Body lying semi-recumbent, facing almost due north. Stiff and cold. Right hand grasping revolver: loosely grasping (but better not try to remove it). Wound in centre of forehead, but not much blood. Footmarks? What about footmarks? They were always important. In the soft, peaty soil in the neighbourhood of the stacks two sets of footprints were clearly visible, his own and the dead man's. In one place he saw the faint indent of a lady's shoe, doubtless Miss Conyer's. He verified the fact of the footprints being those of the dead man by taking an imprint of his boot on a sheet of paper, cutting it out, and comparing it with the marks left in the spongy soil. He noticed too that these marks were deeper than his own, though the dead man was considerably lighter than he was. But then presumably the footprints were made after the rain of last night, when the ground was soft.

Was there anything else he could do? Perhaps it might be a good thing to measure the man's stride. He had no measuring rule in his pocket, but he knew that his span covered exactly eight and a half inches. Kneeling on the turf, he made his calculations and was proceeding to jot them down on paper, when he caught sight of what looked like minute fragments of wood. He picked up nearly a dozen, which he examined carefully with his lens, but he could make nothing of them. It almost seemed as if someone had chosen this spot to sharpen a pencil, yet there was about them no trace of lead. Probably they signified nothing; but he none the less tucked them carefully away in the corner of the envelope that contained the prospectus of the Central Sumatra Consolidated Rubber Company. And now it was time to be going, if he were not to wear out Miss Conyer's patience.

He found her sitting in the heather, lost in thought.

"There's nothing we can do," he said, "except notify the police and, I suppose, a doctor."

"Before we do that, I have a request to make. Do you think you could keep my name out of the forefront of this affair? I've been passing through a rather difficult time these last few months; that was partly why I came down to Deepdale End for rest and quiet. Frankly I shrink from the publicity of an inquest with my name in all the papers. Could we arrange that it was you who discovered the body?"

"I don't see why we shouldn't," said Mr. Digby. "I could truthfully say that I came across it while walking over the moors. Yes, you certainly shall be spared the necessity of giving evidence, my dear lady. But I noticed that you left one or two tell-tale footprints. Those must be obliterated or we shall be having you accused of murder. My story will be this, and it will be perfectly truthful. After finding the body, I met you and left you in its vicinity, while I went to telephone to the police. If I cannot obliterate all your footprints and if later they happen to be discovered by the police, they will be accounted for by your being left to guard the body while I was away."

"Mr. Digby," said Diana Conyers, with a smile, "you are an arch-conspirator."

He went back to the peat stacks, found the few marks of her shoes, and stamped out their impression with his heavy boots.

"And now about getting on to the police," he said. "Where is the nearest place from which I can telephone?"

"Gaunt Lodge; it can't be more than a quarter of a mile away. I'll stay here until you come back and then go home."

Mr. Digby set off across the moor in the direction she indicated. He soon found himself on a rough track that led down a gully on to lower grassy slopes. He walked quickly, and five minutes after leaving Miss Conyers he was ringing the bell at Gaunt Lodge. He explained his errand to Mr. Stillwinter and lost no time in putting through his messages to the Keldstone Police Station and Dr. Jacobs's surgery. He had half hoped that Jim would be there, but it was the querulous, slightly flustered voice of the old doctor that replied to him. He would be at the scene of the tragedy in half an hour and would bring the police with him.

"Well, that's that," said Mr. Stillwinter. "You've time at least for a quiet drink. Better have a small whisky and soda, Digby. This sort of thing is apt to shake one up. And you need not fear interruption from our friend Mr. Wake," he added, as they sat down in the verandah. "I am thankful to say that that economic paragon (between us two a little of him goes a long way), if omniscient, is not omnipotent. He cannot throw a stone straight, and what is more, he confessed as much himself. He was up before breakfast, it seems; saw a mangy-looking tom-cat climbing up the ivy;

chucked a pebble at it, and broke the pantry window. He has cycled over to Keldstone to fetch a plumber. Plumbers in our part of the world, you must know, have no use for telephones. News of a burst pipe must be broken to them very gently, usually at second or third hand. And now tell me all about this sad affair."

Mr. Digby stayed for a quarter of an hour at Gaunt Lodge and then made his way slowly back to the scene of the tragedy. He found Miss Conyers waiting for him, but as soon as he had assured her that there was nothing more that she could do, she left for Deepdale End.

"I am more than grateful, Mr. Digby," she said, "for your help."

They shook hands.

"Miss Conyers," he replied, with old-fashioned courtesy, "you can always command my services."

Diana Conyers had not been gone five minutes, when he saw three men approaching across the moor. Inspector Walters led the way. He was followed by Dr. Jacobs and a police constable, who was carrying a stretcher.

"You are Mr. Wrigley, I suppose," said the inspector, brusquely. "Well, suppose you tell me what you know of this, while the doctor here verifies the fact of death. You, Saunders, put the stretcher down there. I'll want you later."

He took out a note-book and put a stub of pencil to his lips.

"My name is Athelstan Digby, Justice of the Peace for the West Riding. I'm senior partner of the firm of Digby, Dyson and Coppleston."

Mr. Digby was a modest man, but he was a Yorkshireman,

who took himself seriously. He saw no reason why he should not impress at the outset this rather bumptious official with a sense of his importance.

He told his story shortly and lucidly.

"Thank you, Mr. Digby," said the inspector, closing his note-book with a snap. "I'm much obliged; and I don't think I need detain you further, though I'm afraid you will be required at the inquest. Present address? Mr. Lavender's in the High Street. And now, doctor, if you've finished, I'll have a look at things a little more closely."

Inspector Walters turned his back on Mr. Digby. It was evident to that gentleman that he had received his dismissal and that his presence was not required. Should he say anything about his own investigations? Why should he? Let the surly fellow use his own eyes and make his own deductions. It was what he was paid for. But at the risk of a rebuff he would ask about the dead man's identity.

"Do I know him?" said Inspector Walters, who was kneeling by the body. "Why, yes, I do. He's Alf Petch of Worpleswick. He and his wife do for the Reverend Offord. How he comes to be here is another matter, though. You'll learn more about that at the inquest, Mr. Digby. Good day, sir, and much obliged."

Obviously there was no use in his waiting and, with a nod to Dr. Jacobs, he set off home. Stillwinter, he knew, would have been glad to give him lunch, but he did not want to talk. There was too much to think about. Foxy's name was Petch and Petch was Offord's servant. Petch and Offord had wanted the same book, presumably for the same reason. And now Petch didn't want it any more, because Petch was dead. But who killed him? Did he kill himself? And where did the whistling chauffeur come in? There were many queer questions for Mr. Digby to answer.

V

Who Is Neville Monkbarns?

As soon as he had finished lunch, Mr. Digby turned once again to the problems that faced him. The starting-point was the afternoon of the day before yesterday, when three men asked for *Mr. Badman*. The book was the centre of attraction. Around it Jim had woven his ingenious theory of the wager. That, however, would no longer hold. It was not death-proof. Yet, Mr. Digby was convinced that the book contained the clue to the mystery.

He took down the volume from the shelf and proceeded to scrutinise it more carefully than he had done before. There might be some marginal comment on one of the pages, unnoticed in a cursory examination. He turned them slowly, leaf by leaf. More than once he found that the pages were slightly adherent, as if the book had been kept tightly wedged between other volumes in a damp room. Then he came across two pages, two edges of which were so closely stuck together that he had turned them over as one before realising his mistake. He was on the point of separating them with his paper-knife, when he noticed a thin single sheet of note-paper that lay between them. Mr. Digby's fingers shook with excitement as he picked it up.

The letter was written in a thin, boyish scrawl.

"*March 13, 1913.*
"*Somewhere in Sydney, better not say where.*

"DEAR FATHER,
    "*I am sending you a little book which may amuse you and which certainly is appropriate. The idea of shipping me out here was pretty futile, though I don't blame Lady M. for wanting to get rid of me. It's quite natural that she should want to see the black sheep fleeced, and you can bet they've done it. You won't hear from me again, not at least by letter. I've adopted another name, having successfully smirched yours and mine. If you ever hear of Neville Monkbarns (and it's to be hoped you won't), that's me; in other words your slightly resentful son Richard Mottram. (Poor old Dad.)*"

Mr. Digby read the letter three times and then put it back in the book. Richard Mottram, Neville Monkbarns. Both names were familiar. Sir Richard Mottram was the Home Secretary, the ablest man in the Cabinet, whom everyone predicted would go far in politics. Was it to him that the letter was written? He had a vague idea of having heard that he had married twice. Lady M. presumably would be the young fellow's stepmother.

But Neville Monkbarns? Where had he seen the name? In the papers somewhere, and quite recently. It wasn't the sort of name you would forget. Was it in connection with the films? A silly, theatrical sort of name! He had a vague recollection of newsboys crying it in the fog in Bradborough streets. Perhaps he would remember it in time; perhaps Jim would know. In any case there was a new explanation to the problem—or rather, a very old one—blackmail. The letter was a proof, at least with other evidence it would be a proof, of the identity of the son of Sir Richard Mottram with one Neville Monkbarns.

Mr. Digby closed the book and, picking up his hat and stick, almost ran downstairs. He was brimful of facts and theories that demanded an intelligent hearer. He must find that nephew of his and learn what he had to say about it all.

Jim was in the garden at the back of Dr. Jacobs's house, stretched full length under the shadow of Dr. Jacobs's cedar.

"If his cedar ever becomes my cedar," he said, as he rose to get a chair for his uncle, "I shall underprop the boughs. The tree is one of the finest I've seen, and yet the old man grudges it crutches. I wonder how he would like to be caught out in a March snow-storm without a walking-stick. But to-morrow I shall be free from servile bonds of hope to rise and fear to fall. We will start our holiday in earnest. My bags are packed. Even now the good Mrs. Lavender is busy airing her second-best bedroom. The tents of Jacob are the house of bondage."

"Hard labour beneath the cedar," said Mr. Digby, smiling. "I think I understand now what the agent meant by an unopposed country practice."

"Appearances are against me," Jim went on; "but as a matter of fact I was up the greater part of the night. Bryden, the gamekeeper, was taken suddenly ill and I had to motor him in to Maltwick to be operated on. Then, when I got back, there was the morning surgery and two emergency calls besides the usual round. Old Jacobs, of course, was busy with the police. I shall have to help him with the post-mortem. You should have heard the tactful way in which he has been pumping me on the question of medical jurisprudence. I want to hear all about what happened this morning, Uncle."

"You certainly shall, my boy. There are a number of things that I want to straighten out in my mind, and a detailed narrative of what I have been doing to-day will certainly clear the ground. There are two parts to the story and I look to you to supply the sequel."

"Then we will have Act One now, followed by an interval for light refreshment. Jacobs is out, so that we shall be undisturbed. If you'll excuse me for one minute, I'll tell Molly that we will have tea in the garden."

As soon as he returned, Mr. Digby began his story. He omitted no detail, and brought out from his pocket his pencilled notes and the envelope in which he had placed the little chips of wood. Jim proved an excellent listener, and for the first time that day Mr. Digby received the impression that his comments were being taken seriously.

Part One concluded just as the maid brought out the tea.

"Before I begin Part Two," said Mr. Digby, as he helped himself to sugar, "there are a few questions I want to ask you. What do you know of Sir Richard Mottram?"

"He's the Home Secretary and Diana, Miss Conyers'

stepfather. I've only met him on three occasions. I thought him rather cold and reserved, but in the circumstances it was perfectly natural. You knew, of course, that Deepdale End belonged to him, though he is usually only there for the grouse-shooting."

Mr. Digby's eyes opened in amazement.

"Miss Conyers' stepfather and the owner of Deepdale End! You have been taking my knowledge too much for granted, Jim. And when, might I ask, did you first become acquainted with that young lady?"

"During the war. She was a V.A.D. in one of the hospitals at Abbeville. I haven't seen much of her since. What was the other question you wanted to ask?"

Mr. Digby chuckled to himself. He was beginning to see a new light on his nephew's liking for Keldstone, the secretive young dog!

"The second thing I want to know," he said, "is where and in what connection have I heard the name Neville Monkbarns?"

It was Jim's turn to chuckle.

"Dear old uncle," he said, "it's quite obvious you don't read the evening papers, to say nothing of the police-court news in the morning editions. Neville Monkbarns is that wastrel who should have been hung for murder and is now kicking his heels about in the lap of luxury at Eastmoor. You surely remember the rumpus the Labour papers made when he was reprieved. One law for the rich and another for the poor; you know the sort of thing. And in this particular instance they were in my opinion perfectly right, and Sir Richard Mottram perfectly wrong."

Of course, Mr. Digby remembered now. The Madingley Mansions' shooting case. Jim had no difficulty in recalling the details of the sordid story. The young film actress, or so she described herself, had been shot in her rooms by Monkbarns in a furious fit of passion. Both, it appeared, were drug addicts. The murder was unprovoked. On the face of things there appeared to be no extenuating circumstances. Monkbarns, who, rumour said, was well connected, was a professional dancer in night clubs. He had fought in an Australian contingent during the war and had suffered from shell shock. That seemed to be the only reason for his reprieve. In Jim's words it was an inexplicable miscarriage of clemency.

"And now," he said, "for the Second Act of the drama."

As Mr. Digby described the details of his discovery of the afternoon, the faces of both grew grave. It was clear that they were concerned with some form of blackmail, with the makings of a political scandal that might easily terminate the career of one of the best-known politicians of the day. The full realisation of all that it implied affected Jim more deeply than his uncle. The man was Diana Conyers' stepbrother. What, he wondered, did she know of all this sordid business? It was a shock to him to think of Sir Richard Mottram, whom he had always pictured as a cold and upright statesman, as a man who could put personal interest before duty. But was that the right way of looking at it? After all he knew very little. There might well be extenuating circumstances. Surely their first concern was to prevent this vile attempt at blackmail.

"I've time to come back with you to the Lavenders," he

said, "before the evening surgery. I'd like to see that letter for myself. Later in the evening Jacobs wants me to examine the body with him and, if the order has come through from the coroner, to help him with the post-mortem. But, thank goodness, to-morrow I shall be free! Then we can play our own hand. In the meantime we must keep any discoveries about Foxy's death to ourselves. If too much truth gets out of the bag, Sir Richard may find himself in the devil of a mess."

"Yes," said Mr. Digby, "for the time being we must hold an unofficial watching brief, both for him and Miss Conyers."

They had not much to say as they walked to the Lavenders', though they had much to think about. Mr. Digby led the way up to the sitting-room, but as soon as he had opened the door, he stopped.

"Hullo!" he said, "what's this? I could have sworn that I left the book on the table."

There was no book on the table. Where it had lain was an envelope addressed to himself. Hurriedly he tore it open and read the letter, while Jim looked over his shoulder.

"DEAR MR. DIGBY," he read,

"It was a great disappointment to me to find you out when I called this afternoon to learn what you could tell me of this sad tragedy. Poor Petch, with all his faults, was a good and faithful servant. He had trouble in his life of which few were aware, and I cannot but think that in a moment of madness he took upon himself the awful responsibility of destroying something which was not his own. Our lives are given *to us, we know not why; but surely we must hope and believe that we are here for the service of each other and that none can be spared. We must think of poor Petch with charity, remembering that it is not for us to judge.*

"Yours very sincerely,
"Percival Offord.

"P.S.—I see that you have found for me the book I ordered. I am taking it with me in order to save you the trouble of postage. If you could drop me a line to inform me how much I owe you for it, I should be obliged. Needless to say, I should be delighted to see you any time that you are in the neighbourhood of Worpleswick."

"I hardly know what to say," said Mr. Digby.

"I do," Jim replied. "I'm damned. The consummate impudence of the man. He waits until you have left the house, tells the servant-girl, I suppose, that he will write you a note, pockets the book, and then indulges in this unctuous composition, his colossal tongue in his colossal cheek."

"I shall never forgive myself for leaving that book about," said Mr. Digby. "It was crass carelessness. And the worst of it is that the man has acted within his rights. I did give him some sort of a promise to keep the book for him, if I should come across it."

"I don't think anyone can blame you," said Jim. "If you had known all that you did after our talk together, you would have acted differently. In the meantime there is this consolation. You put the letter back, you said, in the book, where you found it. There is no reason why Offord should suspect that we know of its existence. He must never guess that we know. After all, there is something to be said for giving a rascal plenty of rope. Sooner or later he will take a leap in the dark."

"And then," said Mr. Digby, with a grim smile, "the vicar of Worpleswick will be suspended."

"Well, I'm hanged," laughed Jim. "I always thought that you were a man of peace."

"And so I am, my boy. But I don't think that it is you that will be hanged, Jim. With Mr. Offord, however, the case is somewhat different. With Mr. Offord—but perhaps it is wiser not to prophesy."

VI
Triple Alliance

AT NOON ON THE FOLLOWING DAY THE TWO MEN HELD a council of war in Mr. Digby's sitting-room. Jim had to report on the post-mortem examination, at which he had assisted Dr. Jacobs.

Dr. Jacobs himself was convinced that it was an ordinary case of suicide. They had found the bullet embedded in the skull and, though flattened, it corresponded with those in the undischarged chambers of the revolver. There was no visible singeing of the flesh around the wound of entry, as would certainly have been found if the barrel of the pistol had been held close to the forehead. It might, however, have been fired by Petch at a distance of two or three feet without producing any singeing of the skin. The pistol had been found loosely grasped in the dead man's hand. In a case of sudden death Pickering said he would have expected it to be tightly grasped, but again there were plenty of precedents to the contrary. If there was an adequate motive for suicide—and for that they would have to await the inquest—his own view was that Dr. Jacobs was probably right in his conjecture. Jim had, however, been struck by one peculiar circumstance. Scattered over the rough tweed coat the dead man had been wearing he had noticed a number of coarse grey hairs about an inch and a half to two inches long. He might have picked them up from a hearth-rug or from some fur-lined coat. There was nothing strange in that. What did puzzle him, however, was the fact that there were at least four or five similar hairs on the man's socks underneath his boots. Dr. Jacobs, who was short-sighted and never liked having things pointed out to him, had made light of the matter, but Jim had managed unobserved to place the hairs in an envelope for further examination.

But what in the meantime were they to do? How far would they be wise in keeping the knowledge they had acquired to themselves? The most obvious thing seemed to be to bring the whole matter before Sir Richard Mottram, since, as Jim remarked, it was his funeral. But before doing that, would it not be well to find out more about the way in which the book had come into the possession of young Samuel Johnson, the son of the gardener at Deepdale End? Diana Conyers was the only person who could confirm his story and she might easily be the possessor of information which would throw new light on the mystery. It would, however, be a cruel thing to involve her in the tragic and sordid affair if she were ignorant of her stepbrother's identity. Mr. Digby thought she was not. He remembered her speaking of having passed through a difficult time; he recalled her reluctance to appear at the inquest as the finder of the dead body. The poor girl might well be anxious to escape from death and thoughts of death.

"We had better see her," said Jim. "You can talk to her first alone and you will soon be able to judge how much she knows. If matters are as you think, we can then discuss together what is the next step to take."

There remained the question of the Reverend Percival Offord. He had the book and his title to it was good. Even if he could be persuaded to return it, he would keep the letter. To try and look for the letter in Worpleswick Vicarage would be like hunting for a needle in a haystack.

"All the same," said Jim, "I should accept his invitation to call. You may learn something more of his character and habits. His acquaintance must certainly be cultivated."

They set off for Deepdale End at half-past three in a car hired from Carter's Garage at the back of the "Golden Crown."

The house was situated some six miles out of Keldstone. Originally an isolated moorland farm, it had been enlarged to form a shooting-box, while still retaining much of its former character. Weathered tiles and grey stone walls conveyed the same impression of warmth and strength as the heather-covered hills that enfolded it.

Miss Conyers was at work in the garden as they drove up, cutting the dead blooms from the roses. She put down her basket and went to meet them.

"How kind of you to call," she said in friendly fashion, as she shook hands, "and how long it seems since the day before yesterday, when we met at the Stillwinters'. I want to know all you can tell me about that poor man."

"That, Miss Conyers," said Mr. Digby, "was the reason why we came. You see I am a poor hand at a compliment. But

I thought you should be informed as to how matters stand, and Jim, who had to see young Samuel Johnson, offered to motor me over. Will you excuse him for five minutes, while I undertake the preliminaries of the story?"

"He'll find the young urchin over in the orchard," said Diana Conyers, laughing, "and Dr. Pickering's diagnosis, I think, will be green apples."

She led Mr. Digby to a verandah on the southern side of the house, where there were easy-chairs and a low table, on which was placed a great bowl of wild flowers, foxgloves, wild columbine from the woods, and purple scabeus. As she sat there in her cool, clean, sensible dress—that is how Mr. Digby would have described it—her brown hands stroking the rough hair of her Irish terrier, her eyes shaded by the broad brim of her garden hat, he felt in his bones that this girl was all right. If he were tactless, she would understand and forgive him his lack of tact.

"Miss Conyers," he said, "I am an old man, almost a stranger, but one who has your best welfare at heart. When we met the other morning on the moor, you said you had had much to trouble you lately. It must seem an impertinence to ask, but, believe me, the matter is important. Was that trouble connected in any way with your family?"

A look half of surprise, half of fear came into the girl's eyes. She said nothing, but inclined her head.

"And was it connected with your stepbrother?"

"Oh, Mr. Digby," she cried, "what do you mean? What do you know?"

"My dear," he answered, as he took her hand, "I think I know what you have suffered. You must pull yourself together and remember that in Jim and me you have friends in whom you can trust. Chance put us in possession of your secret, and we are here this afternoon to consult with you how best it can be guarded; for others, I am afraid, have discovered it who mean to harm your father. I thought it easier to speak to you alone, and while Jim is away I will tell you the strange story of the last few days. Then, if you tell us as much as you feel you rightly can, we shall be able to put our heads together and decide what is to be done."

"Now," he said, when he had finished, "I think you are in possession of all the facts. I cannot say how sorry I am, Miss Conyers, that an act of mine has helped to bring this trouble upon you."

"You mean the loss of the book and letter? No one could blame you for that. It's most awfully good of you to help like this. And now I'm going in to see about tea. Also," she added, "to try and compose my mind."

At tea Jim was wise enough to do most of the talking, and he was quite content that no one should pay much attention to what he said. But as soon as they had finished, the three settled down to serious business.

"I think that first of all," said Mr. Digby, "we ought to hear what Miss Conyers can tell us about the book and how it came into the possession of Samuel Johnson."

"It was like this," she began. "Last week I had a letter from my mother in London, suggesting that I should go through the library here and put aside books that we didn't really want. They have a horrible habit of accumulating and both she and I sit loose to our possessions. I hate being mastered by things. So I made a rather ruthless sweep of the shelves and made three piles of the volumes I discarded. One was to go to the Women's Institute, one to the village reading-room at Worpleswick, and the rest to young Sam to see what he could get for them at Mr. Lavender's. If you hear of the Women's Institute movement not always being successful, it's partly because people treat it like that. They had *Stepping Heavenward, Jessica's First Prayer*, and *A Peep Behind the Scenes*; oh! and a spare copy of *Little Women* too. That must be put down in my defence. I asked Mr. Offord to come over and go through the books I had set aside for the village club."

"What is your impression of him?" said Jim.

"I've never liked the man. He's shifty and ingratiating. He once tutored my stepbrother for his Little Go, and in my opinion did him no good. He has had one or two serious quarrels with my stepfather, and always tries to stick a spoke in his wheel in connection with parish matters. No, we all dislike the man.

"Mr. Offord called early on Tuesday morning. I was out at the time, but when I came in, I walked straight into the library. I remember now that he was poring over a book, but he put it down as soon as I entered the room on top of one of the piles and we exchanged a few remarks. He said that the books would be very much appreciated at the club and that he would tell Petch to call for them. When he had gone, I tied up the three bundles, gave Sam his, and told him that he would probably get several shillings for them at Mr. Lavender's. It seems obvious that Mr. Offord in his confusion put *Mr. Badman* on the wrong pile."

"I think I begin to see light," said Jim. "Offord discovered the mistake he had made and sharply cross-questioned Petch. He may even have suspected Petch of stealing the book. He knows that Sam will bring his bundle to Mr. Lavender's and so calls at the shop. Petch in the meantime has been putting two and two together and inquires for the book on his own account. But I don't see where the whistling chauffeur comes in. Whom does he represent?"

"Why couldn't Offord have commissioned him?" said Mr. Digby. "He couldn't very well make a second visit to the shop in person so soon after the first."

"I suppose that's the natural explanation. But there may be a shadowy third in this business. We mustn't overlook that possibility. In the meantime, we must try and trace the chauffeur."

"I have been wondering," said Mr. Digby, "how and when we ought to inform Sir Richard Mottram of what has happened. Ought we to wait until after the inquest—"

"They've fixed that for to-morrow," interrupted Jim.

"—or ought he to know at once?"

"I think the sooner he knows the better," said Diana. "I could go up to town to-morrow, leaving you to watch proceedings here and to take whatever steps you think necessary. It wouldn't be safe to write. I know my father gives his secretaries a pretty free hand in opening envelopes."

They agreed that her plan would be the wisest. It seemed best, too, after talking the matter over, for Jim not to appear at the inquest. Offord would be there and the two men had not yet met. There were obvious advantages in Jim remaining unknown to him. Dr. Jacobs had officially conducted the post-mortem and from Jim's knowledge of the man he felt sure that he would be glad to monopolise the limelight.

There remained the far more difficult problem of how to keep a watch on Offord. What did he intend to do with the incriminating letter? Would he keep it or pass it on to someone else? It was Diana who provided the only practical suggestion. The verger's wife at Worpleswick, Mrs. Cornaby, had formerly been cook at Deepdale End. She was devoted to Diana and had a deeply rooted distrust of the vicar, whom she firmly believed to be a Jesuit in disguise. Gladys Cornaby, aged sixteen, was engaged as a daily help at the vicarage.

"I'll go round there this evening," she said, "and tell her that I believe Mr. Offord has got some scheme on foot against my father. She'll think of it in terms of vestments and candles and secret appeals to the Bishop; and I'll ask her to report his doings to Mr. Digby, who is a pillar of Protestantism."

"You can truthfully say that I am on the Board of the British and Colonial Bible Society."

"That's excellent. You can call on Mr. Offord and ask him to take the chair at a meeting which you thought of getting up, to be addressed by the Wesleyan minister. He will refuse, and Mrs. Cornaby will be absolutely convinced of your *bona fides*. She will be drawn to you by the strongest of prejudices, religious and personal."

"If you go on like this, Miss Conyers, I shall have to resign from the Board in your favour. I must condole with you on your extraordinary knowledge of the world. I should never have thought that you were such a diplomatist."

VII
What Twelve Men Thought

THE INQUEST WAS HELD IN A ROOM AT THE BACK OF the "Faversham Arms." There were fewer people there than Mr. Digby had expected. His mind had been so full of the strange events connected with Petch's death, that it came almost as a shock to realise that to the onlookers there was nothing extraordinary in the proceedings; that to the officials it was all part of the day's work. Offord occupied a seat not far from his own. He gave a nod to Mr. Digby and then continued talking in a low voice to a stout red-faced woman, dressed in black, who, Mr. Digby supposed, was the widow. The only other persons he recognised, apart from Inspector Walters and Dr. Jacobs, were Daniel Lavender and Mr. Olaf Wake, who was busy polishing his rimless glasses.

The coroner, a wizened little old man, opened the proceedings, after which the jury and witnesses adjourned to view the body. On their return Mr. Digby was sworn and proceeded to give his evidence. His narrative was short and to the point and elicited no questions from the coroner. Mrs. Petch was then called. The coroner addressed a few words of sympathy to her and told her to remain seated while he asked her a few questions. Mrs. Petch drew a large handkerchief from her handbag and began to sob.

"Tell me," said the coroner, after she had answered almost inaudibly the preliminary questions, "had you noticed anything wrong with your husband recently?"

"Nought to speak on, your worship. He'd the influenza a couple of months back and took a bit of time to pick up; but he was well enough come Tuesday last."

"And what did you notice then?"

"Nought to speak on. He seemed a bit worreted and wouldn't keep still. He was out all day and wouldn't touch his food."

"Had he anything to worry him at home?"

"He was always worrying. He's never been the same since our Gertie left and that was over twelve years ago."

The inspector whispered something to the coroner, who nodded his head.

"I don't want to go into a painful matter more than is necessary," he said. "I take it that the conduct of your daughter was a cause of deep grief to your husband. Is that so?"

Mrs. Petch nodded her head.

"Had he referred to it recently?"

"He said only on Tuesday that he'd get even with them that was the cause of it."

"Was there anyone who wished him ill? Had he enemies?"

"No, your worship; there was nothing beyond back-biting. No one seemed to take notice of poor Petch."

"One other question, Mrs. Petch. Was he, as far as you know, in possession of a revolver?"

"I never saw him with one. He'd a gun for the rabbits, and a licence, but I never saw him with a revolver. He was secretive, though, and if he had one, as like as not he would never have told me of it."

The Reverend Percival Offord was then called. Petch had been in his employ for the last fifteen years. He was a good servant, but morose and taciturn. He had noticed that on Wednesday last he had seemed both excited and depressed. He had said something about having done with it all, but at the time he attached no significance to the words.

Inspector Walters then gave evidence. He spoke of the way in which the body was lying, of the revolver grasped loosely in the right hand, of the single track of footprints on the peaty turf, which corresponded with the imprints of the dead man's boots. He gave a list of the articles in the dead man's pockets, which included a watch and over ten shillings in silver. The revolver was of American make. Only one chamber had been fired.

Dr. Jacobs then proceeded to give the results of his post-mortem examination. He spoke at some length and the coroner had to ask him to put in ordinary English some of the technical terms he used. The appearance of the wound was consistent with its having been self-inflicted, though he would have expected signs of singeing of the flesh. Their absence, however, would be accounted for, if the revolver had been fired at arm's length. He had found a bullet lodged in the base of the skull. It was one which could have been fired from the revolver produced. From the condition of the body it was his opinion that death must have taken place about twelve hours before it was found or in the early hours of Thursday morning.

The coroner then asked the jury if they had any questions they would like to put. A burly farmer rose in his seat and said he would like to know if anyone could account for the deceased being found by Bramfitt's peat stacks, which were three long miles from Worpleswick as the crow flies and four by road. With a sigh at the unreasonableness of juries, the coroner turned to Mrs. Petch.

"Do you know of any reason that would take your husband in that direction?" he asked.

"No, your worship. If he was out just for a walk, all directions were the same to him."

"We must leave it at that," he said, as he glanced at his watch. "Now, gentlemen, I do not think we need detain you. Your duty is to decide how the deceased met his death. You have heard the medical evidence, which is consistent with the supposition of suicide, though you must not omit from your consideration other possibilities. We know that the deceased had had trouble, which had affected him deeply. Two witnesses have spoken to the fact of his behaviour being unusual on the Tuesday and Wednesday. You will remember that Mr. Offord heard him speak of 'having done with it all.' We know, too, that he had recently suffered from influenza, that mysterious complaint, which is so frequently followed by deep depression. None of the deceased's effects were missing. No traces were found of the presence of anyone with him on the moor."

The jury whispered together for a few minutes and

then the foreman delivered their verdict: "Suicide while of unsound mind."

As Mr. Digby passed out of the room, he felt a hand on his shoulder and, turning, found himself face to face with Mr. Olaf Wake.

"An interesting example of crowner's law," said that gentleman. "I wonder how much longer that venerable institution will survive. They have a far better way of running things in France. I've attended inquests in France, Italy, and Belgium, but never in England until to-day. It's always interesting to see the actual working of the machinery of government. I had hoped while I was with Mr. Stillwinter to attend the local court leet, but I shall probably have to cut short my visit. The court leet, you know, is a relic of the manorial system, and has to do with rights of grazing and turbary. If Mr. Stillwinter wants to cut turfs from the moor, he can do so, but he will be fined. Sir Richard Mottram, on the other hand, can have his turfs for nothing, because Deepdale End embodies an old farm-house, the chimney of which is still standing. Gaunt Lodge, on the other hand, is just a modern excrescence on the face of the moor with no rights and privileges. You are staying, I understand, at Mr. Lavender's? Then very likely we may meet again before I leave. Good morning!"

"A bumptious and rather objectionable young man, and one whom it would be very difficult to catch out," said Mr. Digby to himself, as he entered the door of his lodging.

He found Jim in the sitting-room, poring over a map.

"And what happened at the inquest?" he asked. "I suppose they brought in a verdict of suicide."

"Yes," said Mr. Digby; "but I must say it seemed justifiable. Petch seems to have had some private trouble weighing on his mind. I thought of walking over to Worpleswick this afternoon to see what I can find out from Offord. And how have you been occupying the morning?"

"I've just got back from the moor," said Jim, "where I've been examining the scene of the tragedy. Of course the footprints were pretty well obliterated by now, but none the less it was well worth while. The more I think of it, the more I feel sure that, in spite of the jury's verdict, we can't put murder out of court, even though the chances against it are one in a hundred. Take the question first of motive. We know that Petch and two other men, of whom Offord was one, were anxious to get hold of a letter containing a most important piece of information. Their object presumably was blackmail. The man who offers you the alternative of your money or your honour is often a potential murderer. Then again, what was Petch doing that night on the moor three or four miles away from home?"

"That was the very question one of the jurors asked," broke in Mr. Digby.

"And a very sensible question, too, when he could have shot himself in far lonelier places nearer to his home. But suppose he had been given a rendezvous at the turf stacks by the murderer? The place could not have been better chosen. The murderer approaches the spot through long heather, that leaves no trace of his footprints. The heather, too, affords him cover. Petch follows the path up the gully and then crosses the soft, peaty soil, leaving a clearly marked track. When he has reached the last of the stacks, the murderer fires at close range. There was long heather within three or four yards of the spot where the body was found. Finally there is that wood powder that you discovered and those hairs that were so curiously distributed on the clothing. What do they mean?"

"We can do something to settle the latter point," said Mr. Digby. "I'll send them off to-day to young Simpkins. He is assistant director of the Bradborough Woolcombers' Association's laboratory. There's science in our business nowadays, Jim, as well as yours. If anyone can tell us from what beast, two-footed or four-footed, they came, he is the man."

"Why not let him have the powdered wood as well," said Jim, "and see what he can make of it? Have you got it in your pocket?"

Mr. Digby took out the envelope. Jim shook the little fragments out on to a sheet of paper. He scrutinised them carefully with the aid of Mr. Digby's lens, and then, bending over the table, smelt them.

"There's something familiar," he said, "in the scent, though I can't quite place it. It reminds me of an empty cigar box; but that may be because I've only just finished smoking a cigar, the parting gift of old Jacobs."

VIII
High and Low

It was two o'clock in the afternoon, the hottest time in the July day, when Mr. Digby set off for Worpleswick, but, as he walked along the footpath through the fields, he was at first conscious only of the welcome change from the stuffy atmosphere of the back room at the "Faversham Arms." Gradually his pace grew slower, and when he swung his stick, it was no longer an index of exuberance of spirit so much as a register of exasperation. He cut viciously at the thistles in the rough pasture; viciously he prodded the stray pieces of silver paper and orange-peel that littered at intervals the path. He did not like the part he was playing any more than the man he was going to see. He disliked very much the idea of a nice young lady like Diana Conyers encouraging Mrs. Cornaby to spy on the vicar, and when he came to think of it, he was really shocked at her suggestion of using the British and Colonial Bible Society as a pawn in a sordid game. He wondered what the Bishop of Southminster and the President of the Free Church Council, to say nothing of the Reverend Thomas

Tipplewhite, their indefatigable organising secretary, would think, if they had heard her proposal. Did Miss Conyers realise that the Society in one year alone had been instrumental in circulating one and a half million copies of the Scriptures in a hundred and twenty-seven different languages? Surely, he told himself, if she did, a really nice girl—and he was convinced that she was a really nice girl—would not have spoken so flippantly. He himself was much to blame, only he was so fond of young people and listening to their talk, that he was always forgetting the value of a word in season. As to the larger question of whether he was justified in helping Sir Richard Mottram to escape from the results of an action which at first sight no man of honour would condone, Mr. Digby was not seriously troubled. He could imagine the awful conflict when the father was faced with the decision of life and death. He himself had always been an active opponent of capital punishment. Even though Monkbarns was his son, that was no reason why Sir Richard should not have given him the benefit of the doubt. No murderer should be executed; all murder was madness. So at least thought Mr. Digby.

He pulled out his watch. It was three o'clock and he was almost at Worpleswick. He could hardly call on the vicar yet, but there was no reason why he should not spend half an hour or so in the church. He would be sure to find it unlocked. Over a stile and down a shady lane went Mr. Digby, pausing for a few minutes to watch the Saturday afternoon cricket match in progress on the green, up the long straggling street, past the pond, shrunk to a quarter of its winter's size, where white ducks dabbled in the green slime, to where a squat stone tower stood, grey against the elms.

He sat for a moment in the south porch to admire the deeply cut hatchet work of the Norman doorway and the massive hinges of the door. The interior was interesting too, with the cross-legged effigy of William de Worpleswick in the north aisle and the tomb of Sir Jeremiah Singleton, whose kneeling figure faced that of his stone-ruffed lady. It was he, Mr. Digby read in the inscription beneath the tower, who had bequeathed the sum of four pounds yearly to be distributed to poor widows of the parish. He wondered if the good woman who was so busy scrubbing the floor was a participator in the dead man's bounty. Then he remembered. This would be Mrs. Cornaby.

"You have a beautiful old church here," he began. The woman looked up but went on with her scrubbing.

"The church is right enough," she said, "but there's precious few that enters it, and those that do manage to bring in a powerful lot of muck. Oh, you're all right, sir," she went on, as Mr. Digby glanced in apprehension at his feet. "I saw you using the door-mat as you came in. Times have altered since Canon Westover's day. The best preacher this side of Maltwick and a bible-class in the vestry every Wednesday evening. If you wait half a minute till I've done, I'll show you his photograph. It's hanging there now, though there's some what would like to turn his face to the wall."

"He was a fine man," said Mr. Digby. "I knew him years ago at Bradborough and have often taken the chair for him at Bible Society meetings."

"You don't say so, sir? Then you'll be the Mr. Digby that Miss Diana was speaking of quite casual yesterday. It seems that there's more trouble brewing between Sir Richard and

Mr. Offord over these here Romish goings on. I couldn't quite make out what it was all about, but I'll be no party to underhand manoeuvres. It's the Prayer Book they want to revise to-day and it will be the Bible to-morrow; you can take my word for it, Mr. Digby. But I don't think Mr. Offord will steal a march on us this time. Thank heaven, I know a Jesuit when I see one; and if any come poking their noses about Worpleswick, they've got to reckon with me. I haven't forgotten Bloody Mary."

Mr. Digby felt profoundly uncomfortable. He tried in vain to interrupt the flow of Mrs. Cornaby's invective. Every attempt of his to break in was interpreted by that lady as an unqualified assent to what she was saying. Miss Conyers had put him into an intolerable position and he was afraid that he would find it very hard to forgive her. Not for the first time the old Adam in Athelstan Digby told him that a woman's conscience was a very terrible thing. At last he made his escape, and though he slipped five shillings into the offertory box, he had an uneasy feeling that he was vainly endeavouring to purchase an indulgence.

He was reminded again of Mrs. Cornaby and his painful departure from the ways of honest dealing when he rang the bell at the vicarage and the door was opened by a neat little girl, who eyed him with unreasoning suspicion.

"This," he told himself, "will be Gladys Cornaby, preparing to have no truck with Popery."

Mr. Offord, he learned, was at home, and he was shown into the study while Gladys went in search of him. He ought to have been watching the cricket match or revising his sermons for to-morrow, thought Mr. Digby.

He was not impressed by the character of Mr. Offord's study. In the first place there were not sufficient books, and what books there were seemed to be stuck in the shelves without care or arrangement. They were mostly works on mathematics and second-rate novels. There were a few pictures on the walls, some framed and faded photographs of college groups, a rather charming little water-colour drawing of the fen country, a couple of collotype engravings after Marcus Stone, and a large coloured reproduction of the *Mona Lisa*, which hung over the fire-place and was believed by Gladys Cornaby to be the portrait of a Popish saint laughing at Protestants. On the mantelpiece were two silver cups, with a coat of arms that somehow seemed familiar to Mr. Digby. A copy of the *Man in the Street*, the cheapest and most sensational of weekly papers, lay open on the table.

The door opened, and Mr. Offord came into the room.

"So glad you've taken me at my word and looked me up, Mr. Digby," he said. "I tried to get a word with you this morning, but you were busy talking with a friend. Let me settle my debt with you and get *Mr. Badman* off my conscience. How much do I owe you?"

"I'd prefer to take nothing," said Mr. Digby, rather stiffly.

"Oh come, my dear sir, the book is worth five shillings at least. I really must insist."

Very reluctantly Mr. Digby put the two half-crowns in his pocket. He was determined that they should not remain there long.

"And now," said Mr. Offord, "let me offer you a cigarette. Or perhaps you are thirsty after your walk. A little whisky or a glass of beer? You are quite sure? I shall remember you, Mr. Digby, as the man who prefers to take nothing."

"You can give me a little information," he said. "I am naturally interested in the tragedy of poor Petch's death, but I didn't altogether grasp at the inquest this morning what it was that had unsettled his mind."

"No, to be sure. To a stranger the references were not obvious. As a matter of fact our worthy coroner was skating over thin ice and managed to display a considerable degree of tact. Behind those vague allusions lay a painful story; what a rag like this," and he pointed to the *Man in the Street*, "would describe as a scandal in high life. To cut the matter short, the only son of Sir Richard Mottram seduced poor Petch's daughter. I suppose there was wrong on both sides. Perhaps as a man of the world you would prefer to put it that there was human nature on both sides. But the boy treated her badly. She disappeared and died some eight years ago in unhappy circumstances."

"And young Mottram? What has become of him?"

"Young Mottram, Mr. Digby, is, I am afraid, a thorough wastrel. I saw a good deal of him at one time. He stayed with me one summer, while I was coaching him for an exam. There was some good in him, I suppose, but he was idle and dissolute. His father was always being called in to pay his debts, and finally, I believe, he was shipped off to Australia. I should think that probably he was killed in the war under some other name. I have a photograph of him somewhere."

He went to one of the shelves and took down an album.

"That's the boy," he said, "as I first knew him."

It was a snap-shot of a tall and rather lanky youth in riding-breeches.

"A handsome face, though weak," said Mr. Digby.

"Handsome, yes," Mr. Offord went on, "and with unusual features. Some months ago I remember seeing in the papers the portrait of a man—I forget who—that brought poor Dick Mottram most strongly to mind. At times I almost hope that he was killed during the war. If he were alive to-day, he would be doing no good. I picture him as a hanger-on at night clubs and a victim to drugs, one of the pitiful by-products of our civilisation."

Mr. Digby rose to take his leave. He was glad now that he had called, but he felt that he had had more than enough of Mr. Offord's presence.

"I mustn't detain you longer," he said, "and must thank you for the information you have given me. It is a sad story."

"Indeed it is, Mr. Digby, and it is a sad world. These events must have marred your holiday, I fear."

He accompanied Mr. Digby to the door.

"If you have half an hour to spare," he said, as they shook hands, "you might be interested in our little church. I would offer to accompany you myself, but Saturday afternoons are always rather a busy time with me. Good-bye!"

Mr. Digby took the vicar's advice. Those two half-crowns still burned in his pocket and he remembered the offertory box by the door. But once inside the building, he lingered, his feet held by the peace that brooded in the shadows. There, he felt, was something real that had survived the little lives of men. He made his way up the nave and sat down in the fine old Jacobean pew below the lectern. If the church represented the parish, this pew stood for the manor-house, rich and aloof, shut out from prying eyes. He took up a

Prayer Book and read the evening service. Then, turning to the fly-leaf, he saw the name that was written on the pages— Richard Mottram. He had been sitting in the Mottram's family pew. He had forgotten that Deepdale End was in the parish of Worpleswick. How strange, though, that he should be gazing for the second time at the handwriting of the boy whose photograph he had seen only a quarter of an hour ago. For he recognised the handwriting. Without doubt the signature was the same as that appended to the letter which he had found between the pages of *Mr. Badman*.

IX
The Number of the Beast

JIM PICKERING WAS BEGINNING TO WONDER WHAT HAD happened to his uncle. It was after six and there was no sign of him. What could he be doing all this time at Worpleswick? He had just made up his mind to set off in search of him, when he saw Mr. Digby limping slowly down the street and hurried downstairs to meet him.

"I'm all right," said the old gentleman. "No, I haven't been waylaid by the emissaries of *Mr. Badman*. I slipped on a stile in by-path meadow and twisted my ankle."

It was a nasty sprain, but Jim soon had it bandaged and his uncle comfortably settled—as far as a heavy body can ever settle on slippery horsehair—on the sitting-room couch.

"By the by," he said, "you haven't opened your telegram. It came a couple of hours ago."

It was from Diana Conyers. "Returning to-morrow, Sunday. Will get motor at York."

"She must have had a pretty rotten time, poor girl!" said

Jim. "I don't envy her that interview with her father. I only hope she comes back with some practical suggestions, for we don't seem as yet to have got very far. But I've heard nothing yet of how you fared this afternoon."

Mr. Digby told what little there was to tell.

"And now," he added, with a sigh, "I suppose I'm out of the running for a bit. I see myself getting very tired of this sofa, Jim, and the springs don't seem to be as young as they were."

Pickering, however, had an idea. Why should his uncle be confined to the house in glorious July weather, when his car was in the garage at Bradborough doing nothing? If he took the milk train in the morning to York, he ought to be able to reach Bradborough in the early afternoon, get the car, and be back at York in time to meet Diana Conyers. The plan had many things to commend it. A car would increase the range of Mr. Digby's activities and make it much more easy to keep in touch with Deepdale End. Mr. Lavender's railway guide showed, too, that the idea was feasible.

Jim was early astir next morning. A long, slow journey to York, a hurried lunch in the Station Hotel, and then an equally slow and far more tedious three hours in a train that stopped at every station, and he was in Bradborough.

"What a town to leave behind you," thought Jim, when the last tramway standard was passed and granite setts gave place to smooth macadam. Between John Bunyan's City of Destruction and John Bull's City of Construction with its dark Satanic mills there seemed to him little to choose.

At York he met the London train. Diana was there, surprised, and pleasantly surprised he thought, to see him.

"My uncle's car is waiting outside," he said, "but what about some tea first? We have a good two hours' drive before us."

"Tea by all means," said Diana, "and an egg with it, please. I managed to get a cup at Grantham, but half of it upset in the saucer and the rest was the sugared decoction that always reminds me of Sunday School treats."

They found a quiet corner in the refreshment-room.

"I've seen my father," she said. "The whole thing, of course, came as a terrific shock to him. He remembered you, of course, Dr. Pickering, and he's most awfully grateful for your help and Mr. Digby's. He takes a very serious view of things. As you know, he is a well-hated politician. It started, I suppose, when he was in Ireland, pulling other people's chestnuts out of the fire, but he's got new enemies now as well. Father has always made a point of not discussing political matters with me, but I suppose it's common knowledge that there are differences within the Cabinet and that important changes are likely to take place. I believe that father's great ambition is the Foreign Office. If at a time like this his personal honour were called into question, it would mean the end of his political career. A rag like the *Man in the Street*, for example, with that letter in their possession could force his resignation. They always maintained that there was some sinister influence working behind the scenes in the Madingley Mansions' case. I remember some of their beastly placards now.

"Poor father," she went on after a pause. "You've only met him two or three times and I expect he struck you as cold and rather heartless. He isn't really; if he were, he would never have acted as he did. But how could he have done differently? It was the life of his own son that was at stake. Surely he can be pardoned for using the means that were in his power?"

"I expect I should have done the same," said Pickering; "but that means nothing. Moreover my uncle—and there is no man living for whom I have a greater respect—has never breathed a word of adverse comment against your father's action. If Sir Richard had acted differently, he might have been more just, but he would have been inhuman, and there is something wrong about inhuman justice. But had he no suggestion to make that might help us?"

"He says that of course the most important thing is to get hold of the letter. That is the final proof. But he is equally certain that whatever is done must be independent of the police, and at this stage even of private inquiry agents, though there may be points of detail where their help might be sought. He suggested that it might be well to follow up the third man, the whistling chauffeur."

"Yes," said Pickering, "he has always seemed out of the picture, the odd piece in the jig-saw, that won't fit in. I wonder if we could get hold of the number of his car."

They finished their meal and were soon speeding northward across the plain. Very peaceful it seemed in the still July evening and strangely remote from the little world of sordid intrigue in which for the last week they had moved. There in the plain the hay was already in stack; but the country of big farms and wide pastures was soon behind them and once again they were among the hills, thrown up as ramparts to the high moors. They reached Keldstone a little before seven. As Jim swung the car round the sharp corner by the station, he suddenly put on the brakes.

"Look out, you little imp!" he shouted; "what the dickens do you think you are trying to do?"

A small boy picked himself up from the road and, with a shame-faced grin, began to brush the dust from his coat.

"What do you mean by throwing yourself under the wheels like that? If you must lie down, why not try the pavement? As it is, you very nearly returned to the vile dust from whence you sprung, unwept, unhonoured, and unsung."

The smile on the face of the boy slowly vanished.

"If you please, sir, I was only taking the number of the car."

"What is your name, boy?"

"Jonathan Maggs, Paradise Row," he answered, half-crying.

"I am distressed for thee, my brother Jonathan. But jump into the car. It's all right, sonny," he went on. "I'm not going to take you far, only to Mr. Lavender's round the corner, and if you're a good boy, you'll very likely earn half a crown."

"A sudden brain wave," he explained to Diana. "You'll stop and see my uncle? It would give him real pleasure. I want a few words with Jonathan and then I'll join you."

He led the boy into the empty shop and, seated on Mr. Lavender's high stool, began to question him.

"So you collect the numbers of motor-cars?" he said. "And when you've got a number, what do you do with it?"

"I enter it in my book," said Jonathan, proudly, "with the make of the car."

He produced from his pocket a twopenny exercise book, which he had ruled into four columns, headed Date,

Number, Make, Remarx. The latter were infrequent but concise. "Toad throo," read Jim, "A stinker," "paneted scarlet," "driver no bigger than me."

"You're a sharp lad," said Jim, "and sharp lads are the sort that can keep secrets. I want to trace a car that passed through Keldstone on Tuesday afternoon. It was driven by a chauffeur, a cheery-looking chap, and was on its way to Scarborough. Beyond that I know nothing."

Tuesday, the boy explained, wasn't a particularly good day. Saturdays and Sundays were the best. There were only twelve cars that he'd got on Tuesday.

"It wouldn't be that or that," the boy said, pointing to two numbers. "Those are lorries, and the Fords wouldn't be driven by chauffeurs. I don't remember no cheery-looking chauffeur. There's mostly cursing when they sees me. And of course there was lots of cars what passed through Keldstone on Tuesday that I didn't get. I've got to go to school."

"Jonathan," said Pickering, "I'm going to tear out this page and you shall have three shillings. There'll be another three shillings for you, if you can give me any information about that car or its driver. Is it a bargain?"

Jonathan agreed that it was, and the two parted on the best of terms.

In the upstairs sitting-room Mr. Digby and Diana were deep in talk. She had been complaining that there seemed little or nothing for her to do and that through her Mr. Digby's holiday had been spoilt; but as soon as she had heard what had passed between Jim and Jonathan Maggs, she became more cheerful. She insisted that this was a clue on which she could work. It would be a simple thing for Sir Richard to find out the owners of the cars whose numbers Jonathan had noted and where they lived. That was obviously the first step. She would wire straight away in the morning. Then, if necessary, she could go over to Scarborough and make inquiries there.

She got Mr. Digby to write down what he remembered of the chauffeur's appearance. It was little enough. The man, he thought, was of medium height, clean shaven, and as to his uniform, well, it was just a neat, ordinary, chauffeur's uniform. He was positive that he would recognise the man again if he saw him by his cheerful face.

"Oh, and before Jim takes you back," he said, "I may as well give you the slip of paper he handed to me."

Carefully he removed the contents of his bulging breast pocket, and from them he picked out the single sheet of note-paper on which was printed in large characters:

MR. BADMAN
BY
JOHN BUNYAN.

X
The Man in the Street

WITH THE MORNING MILK ARRIVED NEXT DAY A NOTE
to Mr. Digby from Mrs. Cornaby to tell him that Mr. Offord
had unexpectedly been summoned to York on business and
would be travelling by the 10.30 train from Keldstone. Was
it or was it not a move that concerned them? They thought
it was, but were less certain about the steps that ought to be
taken. On the one hand there was an opportunity of searching
the vicarage in Offord's absence, of repeating the little game
that he had played so successfully when he had last called
on Mr. Digby. But they could be sure that he would not have
left the letter lying about. The most they could hope to find
would be some clue to Offord's relations with Petch or to the
third conspirator.

Mr. Digby, however, was averse to the plan. It seemed to
him that it involved an altogether needless risk and would
almost certainly implicate Gladys Cornaby and her mother
in what, to say the least of it, was an underhand transaction.
On the other hand there was nothing to prevent Jim from

seeing what sort of business it was that took Mr. Offord to York. If it were shady business, he could shadow him. Diana Conyers was following up the number of the car, and the reports from Simpkins of Bradborough could not be expected before Tuesday.

As soon as breakfast was over, Jim walked across to the garage and engaged a driver who could start with them in half an hour. His plan was to catch the train at Monkton Bridge, the next station on the Scarborough side of Keldstone. Mr. Digby would see him off, and then the man could take him on to Scarborough and back by Bridlington and the Wolds. What else was there that he could do? His suit of heather mixture was too conspicuous. He had just time to change it for an unobtrusive tweed before the car came round.

They had only a minute or two to wait at Monkton Bridge.

"Don't do anything rash," said Mr. Digby, as they said good-bye. "The only advantage we hold over these villains at present is their ignorance of what little we do know. A slip on our part may only precipitate a crisis. And buy a copy of *Who's Who?* and *Whitaker's Almanack*. We may find them useful before we are through with this business."

Jim took a first-class ticket and selected a seat in a non-smoking compartment. Offord, he felt sure, would travel in a third smoker. As the train approached Keldstone, he settled down behind the shelter of his newspaper in such a way that, though his face was hidden, he could see what was happening on the platform. Offord was there right enough, chatting to old Reuben Harrison, the stockdealer. The only other man he recognised was that queer fish, Olaf Wake, who was nosing round about the bookstall. For a moment he feared that he too might be travelling to York and might thrust his company upon him.

Pickering was only sociable when he wanted to be. He had developed a theory that the more you saw of certain people, the more you understood them, and that the more you understood them, the more you disliked them, and, disliking them, you were not able to do them justice. Olaf Wake, he felt instinctively, was a case in point.

They got to York soon after twelve. Jim waited until he saw Offord get out of the train, and then followed him at a little distance. He passed through the corridor that led to the Station Hotel.

"Got an appointment with someone," said Jim to himself. "I wonder with whom."

Offord made his way through the lounge to the office, Jim keeping within earshot.

"Can you tell me," he heard him say, "if Mr. Smith, Mr. Blakeways Smith, of the *Man in the Street*, has been inquiring for me? My name is Offord."

The girl at the desk glanced down the register.

"Not staying in the hotel," she said. "A Mr. Campion Smith was here last night; a tall gentleman, with a monocle. Would that be your friend?"

"I don't know him by sight, but I hardly think so. He was to meet me here at twelve, so I'll wait a few minutes on the chance of his turning up."

Jim slipped behind a group of veiled and voluble American ladies and looked at his watch. It was a quarter past twelve. Mr. Smith might appear at any moment. He must decide at once how to act. Mr. Digby's words of caution had vanished from his memory. He would have to take a big risk that success alone would justify. He turned sharply on his heel and walked over to the reception clerk.

"I want to see Mr. Offord," he said.

"He's sitting over in that corner by the palm," she answered curtly.

Jim went forward to meet him.

"Blakeways Smith," he said, holding out his hand. "I'm sorry to have kept you waiting, Mr. Offord. I had a call to make in the city and was detained. Let's find somewhere where we can talk without interruption."

"I should suggest the Museum Gardens," Offord replied. "They are only a few minutes' walk away and it will be cooler there than indoors."

"So far, so good," thought Jim. He had successfully taken the plunge, and the waters, deep and cold, were strangely exhilarating. He glanced at Offord and was reassured to see that the man was obviously ill at ease. They crossed Lendal Bridge and passed through an iron gate into the Museum Gardens. There were few people about; a couple of tourists, guide-book in hand, examining the ruins of St. Mary's Abbey, an old gentleman taking a leisurely constitutional, and a tall young fellow, with the look of a down-at-heels actor, who entered the grounds a minute or two after Offord and Jim.

"We'll sit down here," said Jim, "and get to business."

"You got my letter all right," began Offord. "Well, what do you think of the proposal?"

Jim put his hand into his breast pocket and drew out his wallet.

"I could have sworn I had it with me," he said, feigning surprise. "I must have locked it up in the safe at the office. A capacious safe, Mr. Offord, and invaluable, as you can imagine. No, the letter is under lock and key, but, if it's all the same to you, I should like you to go over again the proposals you made."

Quite certainly Mr. Offord was not at his ease.

"I informed you of the letter," he said, "which by chance has come into my possession and indicated the nature of its contents. I am deeply concerned at what I believe to be a grave miscarriage of justice, and I thought that possibly your paper, which has in the past been the means of exposing many scandals, might very suitably take the matter up."

"For a consideration, Mr. Offord?"

"For, Mr. Smith, as you say, a consideration. Perhaps I should add, for a very considerable consideration."

"Before going into that, Mr. Offord, let me remind you that the position may not be quite as easy as you think. I can claim without boasting to be an authority on the law of libel. The *Man in the Street* doesn't often lose an action. Our secret is really that of the good photographers—the extreme care which we give to the making of the exposure, coupled, of course, with a proper understanding of the use of the dark room."

Jim was warming to his part. He was beginning to feel that he could give points to Blakeways Smith.

"In other words," he went on, "we must be absolutely convinced of the *bona fides* of the evidence. As for the dark room, shall I put it that anything you say will not be used against you?"

Without realising it, Jim had succeeded in manoeuvring the other into an awkward position. Offord tried to hide his vexation by lighting a cigarette.

"This is the letter," he said, taking it from his pocket. "No, I don't intend to hand it over to you at present, Mr. Smith. You have very properly reminded me of the question of *bona fides* and the necessity for caution. You see the writing and the signature. Both can easily be verified by documents in my possession. I might consider providing you with a photograph of the letter, but until we have made a deal, I stick to the original."

The thin sheet of note-paper was within a few inches of Jim's fingers. For one moment he considered the possibility of snatching it from Offord and trusting to his heels; but the gate of the garden was shut and the tall, actor-looking man was sitting on the grass not fifty yards away from them. The risk was too great.

"What do you want for it?" he said at last.

"My terms are two hundred pounds, cash down. A cheque is no use for me."

"Those who from time to time have supplied us with information have often made the same remark," observed Jim, who felt a quiet satisfaction in being able to blacken the characters of Mr. Blakeways Smith and the Reverend Percival Offord at the same time. "You haven't, I suppose, approached Sir Richard Mottram in the matter?"

Offord flushed angrily.

"Look here, Smith," he said, "there's no occasion for you to become offensive. If you don't like my offer, you can leave it."

"Come, come, Mr. Offord, my question was perfectly

natural, though clumsily put. What I wanted to ask you was if anyone knew that you had that letter in your possession. If the matter is still an absolute secret, it will be easier and safer for us both."

As Jim asked the question, he kept his eye fixed on Offord's face. It might have been fancy, but he thought that for the fraction of a second the man faltered in his reply.

"No one knows of it," he said, "besides myself."

"So much the better. We can return to the question of terms. Two hundred pounds is a large sum of money."

"Two hundred pounds, cash down, I said."

"Please don't interrupt me. I might be prepared to pay two hundred pounds for the letter and for the other documents that would be necessary to attest its authenticity. If I did, I should propose that one hundred pounds should be paid when you handed it over to me and the balance on publication."

Offord thought for a moment.

"Make it guineas," he said, "and have it your own way. The agreement, of course, will have to be properly drawn up."

"That can be arranged. Now about the question of cash. I have to be in Scarborough on business to-morrow. I go on there this afternoon. By wiring to London I ought to be able to make arrangements to pay you the money by then. Could we meet at twelve, say, in the lounge of the Grand Hotel?"

"Yes, I could manage that," said Offord.

"It's a bargain, then. And now that we've finished our business, what about a drink?"

Jim had been successful beyond his wildest dreams. He

had hooked his fish and, though he had still to land it, he saw no reason why the tackle should not hold. There were, however, one or two snags in what looked like still water. What, for example, had become of the real Mr. Blakeways Smith? It would be more than awkward if he and Offord were to meet on the platform of York Station. Then he remembered that they were unknown to each other. The risk was negligible.

"What time were you thinking of returning to Worpleswick?" he asked over their second cocktail.

"By the evening train. I'm not often in York, not nearly as often as I should like to be."

"Well then, I'll look out for you to-morrow in Scarborough. I'll send off the wire to London now."

The wire which he dispatched from the post-office in Lendal was not to London.

"Digby, c/o Lavender, Keldstone," wrote Jim. *"Excellent news of Percy, but must have hundred pounds in cash by to-morrow morning—*PICKERING.*"*

XI
The Whistling Chauffeur

MR. DIGBY WOKE EARLY. HE HAD SLEPT WELL AND WAS in a thoroughly happy mood. For things at last were moving, and moving in the right direction. His ride of yesterday had thoroughly invigorated him; there was nothing like this mixture of moor and sea air to make a man forget his years. He put his hand under his pillow. Yes, there was the wallet with the twenty five-pound notes. He had been lucky to get them, for when he got back at four and found Jim's telegram awaiting him, the bank was shut, but, thanks to Stillwinter's interview with the manager, that little matter had been arranged all right. Jim had really done splendidly. It was a good idea of his, Mr. Digby thought, to send off his nephew to Deepdale End almost before he had heard his story, and if Diana was the girl he thought she was, she would give him a warm welcome. Certainly he had seemed in no hurry to return.

How sweetly those blackbirds were singing in the orchard down the lane! He would like to see Jim married and settled. The boys would go bird-nesting in the lanes, as he used to, and they would learn to tickle trout, a thing he had always wanted to do. Seven o'clock striking. It would soon be time to be getting up. And then one of the boys would go into the business. Probably he would become a socialist; Mr. Digby would have to reconcile himself to that; but the old radicalism would come out again in the next generation. Those would be his great-great-nephews and nieces. He would like to live to see them, and there was really no reason why he shouldn't. But, of course, it depended on Jim.

A tap on the door. That was his shaving water. They brought it straight from the boiling kettle. Ten more minutes before he need get up, and Mr. Digby, turning his face to the wall, dozed off to sleep again.

Breakfast was already on the table when he appeared in the sitting-room, a little annoyed that for once the younger generation had caught him napping. A disconsolate-looking Jim was standing with his back to the empty fire-place.

"Good morning, Uncle," he said. "I thought our luck was too good to last. We are back again where we were. Perhaps it's even worse than that. But read the paper for yourself."

Mr. Digby took up the copy of the *Yorkshire Morning News* that was lying on the table.

Tʀᴀɢɪᴄ Dᴇᴀᴛʜ ᴏꜰ ᴀ Nᴏʀᴛʜ Rɪᴅɪɴɢ Vɪᴄᴀʀ, *he read.*

"A tragic accident occurred in the centre of York yesterday afternoon, which resulted in the death of the Reverend Percival Offord, vicar of Worpleswick. From accounts given by eyewitnesses, it appears that Mr. Offord was seen in violent altercation with a man on

the pavement outside a hotel in Huckstergate and laid a hand on his shoulder as if to detain him. The man eluded his grasp and made off in the direction of Coney Street, Mr. Offord following. Unfortunately, he failed to notice a heavy lorry, which knocked him down and passed over his body before it could be brought to a standstill. An ambulance was quickly on the spot, but the nature of Mr. Offord's injuries was such that life was extinct before he reached the hospital. We understand that the police are anxious to discover the whereabouts of the man whom Mr. Offord was seeking to detain.

"The deceased gentleman, who was a bachelor, was held in high esteem in Worpleswick, of which parish he had been vicar for the last fifteen years. He was a distinguished mathematician, a former fellow of St. Bardolph's College, Cambridge, and a well-known name in the world of chess."

"The world of chess," said Mr. Digby, "in which he has made his last move. What a terrible occurrence! I hardly know what to make of it."

"I think one thing is pretty clear," said Jim, "and that is, that the letter has been stolen. The man who was trying to get away from Offord was no ordinary pickpocket. If he had been, Offord would have called for assistance. But who was he? I thought at first of Blakeways Smith; but, after all, he is in his way a more or less responsible journalist and could never afford to behave like that."

"It seems to me," said Mr. Digby, as he poured himself out a second cup of coffee, "that we are faced again with the problem of the mysterious third. Three men, and as far as we know, three men only, were anxious to get hold of *Mr. Badman*; and now two of them are dead. If Petch did not commit suicide, who killed him? I must say that I was prepared to suspect Offord; but now I am less sure."

"I don't think Offord was the man," said Jim. "He hadn't got the guts. The only thing we can do now is to get on the track of the chauffeur. There is about one chance in a thousand that Offord's death had nothing to do with *Mr. Badman*. If that is so, the letter is still in his pocket, and probably no one will hear anything more about it. We can't afford, though, to count on that."

"What's the next step, then?" asked Mr. Digby.

"To motor over to Deepdale End and see if Miss Conyers has any news."

Mr. Digby, sitting behind him in the car, felt rather sorry for his nephew. The evening before he had left Deepdale End with all the glamour of assured success; this morning it was no longer his. Instead was cold reality and failure.

One thing he was thankful for. Diana Conyers had already heard the news. Mrs. Cornaby had come over from Worpleswick first thing in the morning. The good woman had forgotten her prejudices and between her sobs had spoken of the dead man's fondness for cats and his skill in handling bees.

She led the way into the library.

"It's an unexpected set-back, isn't it?" she said. "And all the more bitter, when things seemed to be going so well. But I've got a list of the owners of the cars. I've found out, too, from Jonathan Maggs, that he was out of school on Tuesday soon after four. The chauffeur called at Mr. Lavender's between four and five, so that it's quite likely that his car was one of those that Maggs noted."

Diana spread out on the table a sheet of paper, on which were written the numbers and makes of the cars and the addresses of their owners.

CROSSLEY	Wilfrid Pickles, Sunny View, Grimstone Park, Manchester.
ROLLS-ROYCE	Robert Hughes-Jones, The Claverings, Hampstead.
DODGE	Alfred Geary, Clonmel, Harrogate.
MORRIS-OXFORD	Euphemia Upstart, The Inglenook, Easingwold.
OVERLAND	William Grainger, Acomb, York.
MORRIS-COWLEY	John Edward Andrews, 211 Headingley Rise, Leeds.
FIAT	Sir Henry Waterbourne, The Coppice, Hillmorton, Rugby.

"Our best plan, surely," said Mr. Digby, "is to run over to Scarborough and get hold of a list of visitors. If any of these names are among them, we ought soon to be able to find out if they include the employer of our chauffeur. And while we are in Scarborough, we could look too at the visitors' lists of places like Whitby and Filey."

It seemed at any rate the obvious first step. If it were unsuccessful, they could turn to the hotel registers and the garages. They were in Scarborough soon after twelve, secured a copy of the visitors' list and examined it at leisure over lunch. Their bad luck seemed to have turned at last. Hughes-Jones, the owner of the Rolls-Royce, was staying at the "Grand," and among the names of visitors at Whitby was that of Sir Henry Waterbourne at the "Metropole."

"What's the next proceeding?" asked Diana.

"We'll drive round to the garage and ask for the chauffeur," said Jim. "If my uncle recognises him, well and good. If he's not the man, I'll spin a yarn about wanting to look up an old soldier who served under me in the war and whom I understood was working for Hughes-Jones. He'll quite understand, especially when I've tipped him."

It was quite an easy matter to find the chauffeur. The manager of the garage said that he would probably be just round the corner and dispatched a boy to summon him. Unfortunately, however, it was not the man they wanted.

"It was probably my brother Bill," he said. "What name was it you said, sir? Captain Pickering? Many's the time he's spoken to me of you, sir. I'd write and tell him that you've been inquiring after him, but I've mislaid his address. Thank you, sir, I'm much obliged. No trouble at all."

"How much did you give the man?" asked Mr. Digby, anxiously.

"Five bob. You see I recognised him at once as a full member of the Amalgamated Society of Yarn Spinners, and we're bound to stand by each other."

There remained the knightly owner of the Fiat. Jim proposed that they should all drive on to Whitby, but Diana pleaded a headache. She would find a quiet corner in the

Spa gardens, she said, and they could meet her, say, at six at the South Cliff tea-rooms.

She sat for an hour, listening to the music of the band, while from the crowded beach below came the cries of happy children. The bay was dotted with boats. A steam drifter was leaving the harbour, the smoke from her funnel hanging like a black streak across the weather-beaten roofs of the old town, backed by the grand silhouette of the castle and the castle rock, weather-beaten too, but still unconquered.

Diana left her seat. The sun had disappeared behind a cloud and the air was chilly. She was making her way into the town to see about some household purchases, when her eye was caught by a small printed notice in a newsagent's window:

ONE POUND REWARD

The above will be given to anyone who restores to the owner a large black Manx Cat, blind in one eye and wearing a silver collar. Finder should communicate with Miss Euphemia Upstart, Tregennick, South Parade.

Euphemia Upstart! Why, of course, the name was familiar. Once heard, no one would ever forget it. She was the owner of the Morris-Oxford as well as of the black Manx cat that was blind in one eye. Probably she was deaf and the possessor of a large ear trumpet. But it was the chauffeur and not Euphemia that Diana was interested in.

She was soon in South Parade and found "Tregennick"

without difficulty. It was an old-fashioned, red brick residence, standing in its own grounds. A garage had evidently been added recently. Diana, passing the house, walked a little way up the road. She was undecided what to do. At last she made up her mind that she would call on Miss Upstart and ask to be allowed to speak to the chauffeur. If she demanded a reason, she could say that he had once been employed by her father. The moment would bring its own inspiration, and the black cat would surely bring luck.

It was, however, with a feeling of distinct relief that Diana heard the maid's announcement that Miss Upstart was not at home.

"I really came to ask," she said, "if I could speak to her chauffeur for a few minutes. I think it possible that he may know the whereabouts of a book I lost some days ago."

The maid looked at Diana in some surprise. Evidently she was summing her up.

"Oh, I think it will be all right, miss," she said at last. "Lilywhite's round at the back somewhere; I'll go and call him. Will you see him here?"

"I'll wait outside by the garage. I'm so sorry to have troubled you, but the lost book was one I prized greatly."

Diana was not kept waiting long. She heard the back door slam, a laugh, and a man's voice say: "Now don't be jealous, Amelia," and the chauffeur stood before her. As soon as she saw him, she felt sure that their search was over. There was no mistaking the cheerful, half-impudent, wholly honest face, that Mr. Digby had described.

"And what can I do for you, miss?" he said, with a grin.

"Tell me," she answered, "are you the man who went

into Mr. Lavender's bookshop in Keldstone a week ago and asked for a book by Bunyan?"

"The very same," he said; "Lavender and Bunyan! There are some queer names in the world and no mistake; and I've no reason to talk, when they christened me Kitchener Lilywhite."

"It's like this, Mr. Lilywhite," said Diana, with a smile that completely won his heart and made him hope that Amelia was not looking out of the scullery window. "I had a valuable copy of Bunyan's *Mr. Badman*, which was stolen. Three people wanted to get hold of it. Two of them, I know, were unsuccessful, but I haven't been able to trace the third. I wish you would tell me how you came by the paper on which was printed the name of the book."

"It was like this, miss. When we got to Keldstone last Tuesday, Miss Euphemia said that she'd like to stop for tea. I dropped her at Barker's Temperance Hotel, she being always inclined that way, and went on to the 'Faversham Arms,' hostentatiously to fill up with petrol, the weather, you remember, being very hot. In the bar I gets talking to a man, and after a bit he slips a ten-shilling note into my hand and asks me to go across the street and see if they've got that book and to buy it if they have. Well, they hadn't. He tips me two and six and we parts on terms of mutual satisfaction."

"And what was he like?"

"Tallish," said Lilywhite, "and well dressed; wore rimless glasses, clean shaven, hadn't much of a chin, preferred Irish whisky to Scotch, and gave me a dozen good reasons why it was the better. He could talk the hind leg off a horse."

"I'm very much obliged to you, Mr. Lilywhite. The only

other request I have to make is that you will keep this conversation as private as possible. It may be a question of taking public proceedings. If it were, I suppose we could count on you to repeat what you have just been saying?"

"Indeed, yes, miss. It was quite ridiculous, not to say uncalled for, to speak of Irish whisky in the way he did, even if he was right."

"And your address, in case we want it?"

"Kitchener Lilywhite, one 'L,' care of Miss Upstart, The Inglenook, Easingwold, will always find me; but we shall be staying here for the next six weeks. It seems to suit our asthma."

"Mr. Lilywhite," said Diana, laughing, as she shook hands, "you are a wag. Very many thanks for your help. And be sure you make it up with Amelia."

Her headache had gone. She made her necessary purchases and then adjourned to the South Cliff tea-rooms, where she ordered tea, scrambled eggs, buttered toast, and meringues. Soon after six Mr. Digby and Jim joined her. They had had no luck. Waterbourne was one of those unenterprising people who drive their own car.

"And you," said Mr. Digby, "I hope your headache is no worse, Miss Conyers?"

"My headache's gone. I've been far too excited to think about it. I believe I've found out who is Mr. Badman."

They looked at her in utter surprise.

"As far as I can make out at present," said Diana slowly, "it looks as if we should have to concentrate our attention on Mr. Olaf Wake."

XII
Mongolian Goat

DIANA'S ANNOUNCEMENT HAD BEEN RECEIVED BY MR. Digby and Jim with something like incredulity, which in the course of the next twenty-four hours slowly gave place to the conviction that she was right.

Lilywhite's description of the man he met in the bar of the "Faversham Arms" corresponded closely with Olaf Wake. He had talked like Wake and, like Wake, imparted information in such a way that the listener's antagonism was aroused.

Stillwinter, upon whom they called next day, confirmed Wake's preference for Irish whisky. It was, it seemed, a topic on which he was prepared to hold forth at length on the slightest provocation. Wake had been present as a spectator at the inquest; Jim had seen him on the platform at Keldstone on the day Offord had left for York—trifling facts in themselves, but significant, if Diana's hypothesis were accepted. It would have been an easy thing for him to have telegraphed to a confederate in York that Offord was on the train. Then, too, was it coincidence only that Gaunt Lodge, where Wake was staying, was the house nearest to the peat stacks where the body of Petch had been found? Was it a coincidence that he was leaving, indeed had already left, the district? for Stillwinter informed them that he had been called away by telegram on Tuesday evening on important business; and it was on Tuesday afternoon that Offord had met his death.

A perusal of the pages of *Who's Who?* had added considerably to their knowledge. Wake, it appeared, was born in Cork and was privately educated in Ireland and Switzerland. He was a scholar and Fellow of St. Bardolph's College, Cambridge, and was author or joint author of half a dozen treatises on subjects connected with political economy. His hobbies were put down as chess and fencing; his club the Athenaeum. Was it coincidence only, Jim had asked, that Offord, too, was a Fellow of St. Bardolph's and that Offord was an exponent of chess? Did the two men know each other? Had Wake ever called at Worpleswick Vicarage for a friendly game with a man with whose name at least he might be familiar? As far as Stillwinter knew, they had not met, but it seemed that during his visit Wake had come and gone very much as he pleased. He was often out for lunch and always refused sandwiches, holding a theory that most men drank too little and ate too much. In any case it was a question which Mrs. Petch could answer. They decided that they would motor over to Worpleswick after lunch and then go on to Deepdale End to discuss plans with Diana Conyers.

They left before the arrival of the afternoon post. Mr. Digby had expected to have already received the report of the Bradborough analyst in reply to the letter he had sent off on Saturday. Much might depend, everything indeed might depend, on the clues that it furnished. In the meantime they could not do better than increase their knowledge of Mr. Olaf Wake and his doings.

The information which Mrs. Petch was able to give was very much to the point. Wake had twice called at the vicarage. The first occasion was on the Tuesday of the week before, the day when Mr. Digby had kept shop for Mr. Lavender. The second was the morning of Mr. Offord's death. He had called about eleven, at a time when Offord was in the train on the way to York, and had asked to see the vicar. On being informed that he was out, he explained that he had accepted an invitation to borrow some books. Mrs. Petch had left him alone in the study for about a quarter of an hour and on his departure he had handed her a slip of paper on which he had written the names of the volumes he had borrowed. It was still lying on the mantelpiece. Mr. Digby took it up. It had been placed underneath one of the silver cups engraved with the crest that on his former visit had struck him as familiar. He recognised it now as the crest of St. Bardolph's. He had seen it embroidered on the pocket of Wake's blazer on the afternoon of the tennis party at Stillwinter's.

Mr. Digby read the list:

A Critical Survey of the Theory of Relativity.
A Hundred and One Problems in Chess.
Forty Years in a Moorland Parish.

"There is no objection, I suppose," he said, "to my glancing at some of the books on the shelves. If, as I understand, Mr. Offord left no relatives, his library may be disposed of, and there may be one or two volumes that I should like to buy."

"You are quite welcome to look round," said Mrs. Petch, "but, if you'll excuse me, I'll send in Gladys and get on with my work."

As soon as she had left the room, Mr. Digby took down the photograph album that Offord had shown him on his previous visit to the vicarage. Hurriedly he turned the leaves.

"As I thought," he said at last. "That photograph of young Richard is missing and others that I suppose would probably be of the boy as well. Wake would want them for identification purposes."

"What about borrowing it?" asked Jim.

"I don't think we can do that."

"The interest is unusually high," Jim said with a smile. "There may be finger-prints. But as you are a Justice of the Peace, you had better look the other way. I'll act on my own responsibility and, if necessary, I can arrange things later with the executors."

When Gladys Cornaby came into the room a moment later, Mr. Digby was standing with his hands behind his back, gazing out of the window, appalled at the ease with which he was compounding a felony.

It was half-past three when they left Worpleswick. The afternoon post would have arrived, and they decided that it would be worth while calling at Daniel Lavender's for letters before proceeding to Deepdale End.

"Only one for you, Mr. Digby," said Mrs. Lavender. It bore, however, the Bradborough postmark.

"I won't look at it now," he said, as he put it in his pocket. "Diana, Miss Conyers, shall open it. I must confess that there is a certain amount of exhilaration in this business of detection, and we owe it to her not to blunt the edge of discovery."

They had tea together on the lawn at Deepdale End—wild raspberries, which Diana had picked in the woods that morning, and crisp turf cakes from the kitchen fire.

"Now," said Mr. Digby, as he handed Diana the envelope, "let us put our fortune to the test. No, my dear young lady, I can't bear to see a letter ripped open like that. Take my paper-knife. Treat the envelope as if it were the uncut page of a favourite author."

"But I am doing. If the author is exciting and I'm in a hurry, I just bend the pages and pull them apart. We don't go in for hairpins nowadays."

"Miss Conyers, I'm surprised at you. I always pictured you as fastidiously neat in all you did."

"You're wrong then, Mr. Digby, I'm afraid," she answered, laughing. "There now! Even you can't complain of the way that envelope is opened. Shall I read what the man says?"

Mr. Digby nodded his head.

DEAR MR. DIGBY,

I apologise for not having replied to your letter before, but must plead pressure of work. I have made a careful microscopic examination of the hairs which you sent me. They are certainly goat hairs and I think are probably from the Mongolian goat, which was popular some years ago but isn't often met with in the trade nowadays, though it is sometimes passed off as mouflon. The light fawn is the natural colour of the hair. It has not been dyed. I should say that the skin from which the hairs come has not been particularly well preserved. Beyond that I am afraid I can't go. The second specimen you sent for examination is altogether outside my line. It appears to be a mixture of shavings of some soft, open-pored wood, with a few broken fragments of charred twig, possibly ling. In accordance with your instructions I have carefully preserved both sets of specimens.

Trusting that the above somewhat inconclusive report may be of help to you, I remain,

Yours sincerely,
ARTHUR L. SIMPKINS.

"So that's that," said Jim. "It's a relief to know that it's not the common or garden goat with which we have to deal, but his Mongolian brother. We come back again to the ever-present Yellow Peril. A gigantic muster of our moorland flocks is indicated. We must separate the sheep from the goat and then follow where he leads."

"He will probably turn out to be Mr. Olaf Wake's mascot," added Diana.

But Mr. Digby did not smile.

"Anyhow," he said, "we have something definite to work on, a carriage rug, a lined motorcoat, they are things which we might well look out for. But what I want us to decide now is a plan of campaign for the immediate future. Shall we do any good by staying in this neighbourhood? Wake is the villain of the piece and, though he may not have succeeded in covering up his tracks in Keldstone, we may be wasting valuable time by concentrating all our attention here. I think we may take it for granted that sooner or later—and personally I think we shall not have long to wait—he will attack Sir Richard. Don't you think, Miss Conyers, that we ought to consult your father again?"

"I was going to suggest the same thing myself," she said. "Could we all go up to town to-morrow?"

"But there are threads here that still remain to be gathered up," said Jim.

"It certainly is difficult to know how best to act," Mr. Digby went on; "specially difficult when we can't call in the help of the police. How would it be if Jim went up to town with you and tried to get on to the tracks of Wake? We have one great advantage in the fact that he has no suspicion of us, and at the same time, thanks to Stillwinter, we are on the footing of acquaintances. Jim can cultivate Mr. Olaf Wake. We must have a footing in the enemy's camp."

"And what will you do, uncle?"

"For the present I shall stay here. When we were at Gaunt Lodge this morning, Stillwinter suggested that we should move our things over from Daniel Lavender's. It will be natural enough for me to accept his invitation, when I am left by myself. I like the man; I shall be able to discover all he knows about Wake—somehow I don't think it is very much—and possibly at Gaunt Lodge I may come across new clues."

The plan seemed a good one, and when shortly afterwards the two left in the car, it was on the understanding that Jim and Diana would meet at Keldstone station next morning and travel up to London by the 10.20.

"I notice, Jim," said Mr. Digby with a smile, as he bade good-night to his nephew that evening, "that you never suggested your staying with the Stillwinters and that I should go up to London. There is a Board meeting of the British and Colonial Bible Society that I ought to attend on Friday."

"You are forgetting that you have a sprained ankle," Jim replied, "and are under doctor's orders. Bracing country air, freedom from worry, and gentle carriage exercise, that's my prescription."

XIII
A Consultation

"I suppose we are doing the best thing," said Diana next morning, as she settled down into her corner seat. "Somehow I don't altogether like this dividing of forces. Do you think Mr. Digby will be all right by himself at Gaunt Lodge? After all, Mr. Stillwinter was a friend of Olaf Wake's, and I for one don't know very much about him."

"There's no need to worry about my uncle," Jim replied. "There's not very much that escapes his eye, and he's a shrewd enough judge of character, far shrewder than old Stillwinter, for instance, though I fancy even Wake was not quite as successful as he thought he was in the impression he made on him. It's quite on the cards, too, that my uncle may discover something. He has a flair for significant detail. You must get him some time to talk to you about his pictures and the characteristics of his Dutch and Flemish masters. If he feels that he is becoming too positive in laying down the law, he may tell you, for his own discipline rather than for your edification, the story of how he was completely taken in by the Schalken replica."

"I wish he would," said Diana. "There are lots of things I'd like to hear Mr. Digby talk about. He seems to me one of those rare individuals who have the gift of establishing personal relations with all sorts and conditions of men and who in the process has become both wise and kind. I wish I had known him before."

"I expect he shares your wish," Jim answered, with a smile; "but I'm glad you think like that. He's the finest gentleman I know and north country through and through. It's an awful pity, Miss Conyers," he went on, "that your holiday should have been broken into like this. You came down here for a rest, but I'm afraid there's precious little awaiting you in the next few weeks, if I read things aright."

"It wasn't altogether for the rest I came," said Diana. "I love Deepdale End, and the older I get the more I dislike town. I like my slice of life to be of thick home-made bread, not much ham and no mustard; and I want to eat it in a contemplative fashion out of doors, preferably by one of your moorland streams. But, and there always seems to be a but, mother is delicate and my father depends upon me for help, more I think than he imagines. You'll stay with us, of course, while you are in town?"

"I'd love to," said Jim, "but I think it would be better if I didn't. The less we're seen together, the safer we shall be. We must at all costs keep from Wake the suspicion that my uncle and I are working against him. I don't credit him with extraordinary resources, but it's quite on the cards that he has someone keeping a watch on Sir Richard's movements. No, I'll see if they can put me up at my old digs in Bloomsbury and telephone to you this evening. That will give you time to consult with Sir Richard."

The journey for Jim passed all too quickly. Something in what Diana had said—or was it the way in which she had said it?—had removed a weight from his mind. They seemed to be back again in the old days at Abbeville, when he had known her as an unusually competent V.A.D.

He saw her into a taxi at King's Cross and then proceeded to his old quarters. Possibly he was a fool not to have accepted Diana's invitation, but he would be more foolish to underestimate the intelligence of his opponent.

At nine o'clock he telephoned to Warrender Street. Diana answered the call. Her father was out and would not be in till half-past ten, but he was particularly anxious to see Dr. Pickering that night.

"Right," said Jim, "I'll come along."

The three met in the library at Warrender Street. Sir Richard, a tall, lean man, with hair of iron grey and keen dark eyes that seemed to take in everything at a glance, stood with his back to the empty fire-place. His face lit up with a smile as he shook hands with Jim. "It's not the first time we've met, Dr. Pickering," he said, "but it's the first time I've had an opportunity of thanking you for what you have done. I have nothing to hide in this matter from my daughter, Mr. Digby, and yourself. I have no excuse to make. To put the matter frankly, I have used my office and position to save my son. I knew that he was my son; I realised the risk that I ran; and I accepted it. But when I said I have no excuses I went perhaps too far. Dick as a boy was subject to curious nerve storms which the doctors viewed with anxiety. There was insanity in his mother's family. All this if it could have been brought out at the trial, and of course it could not without his revealing his identity, would almost certainly have established the fact that he was not fully responsible for his actions. The boy stood by me, sacrificed himself for me. I ask you, Pickering, if I could have acted differently?"

He was silent for a moment and then went on. "But things are moving rather more quickly than we expected. Lady Mottram received this morning a letter with a type-written slip of paper, requesting her to give the enclosed envelope to me. Here it is; you can read it for yourself."

He handed the papers over to Jim. The outer envelope, addressed to Lady Mottram, was stamped with a West Central postmark. The letter was short and very much to the point.

"The identity of Neville Mottram is known," he read, "and the part you played in securing his reprieve. Unless you resign from the Cabinet before the end of the month, the facts of the case will be published and your career wrecked. The evidence is complete and you would be well advised to take this warning with the utmost seriousness."

"He gives us an interval of ten clear days," said Jim, "in which to call his bluff. Why should he want you out of the Cabinet, sir?"

Sir Richard laughed. "A great many people would rather I was not there," he said, "including some of my own colleagues. The political situation is complicated. Some of us are for a far bolder policy, especially for a bolder foreign policy. We believe that we could carry the country with us, that it is willing to be led but is reluctant to drift as we are drifting at present. On the other hand there are those who counsel delay, who are unwilling to risk the chances of a general election in the near future, and who would use the next two years in spiking some of our enemies' guns. They are pessimists, who say that our party will never again be returned with such a majority and that it is no time for rash experiments."

"And where does Wake come in in all this?" asked Diana.

"I've had a man searching into Wake's record," said Sir Richard, "and the results are interesting. He is half Irish, as we knew already. What we did not know is that two of his brothers were killed, one in Dublin in the Easter week rising, the other two years later, shot by Black and Tans. I suppose at one time I was one of the best-hated men in Ireland, and hate dies hard. There's motive there."

"What did Wake do during the war?" asked Jim.

"He was a conscientious objector. He was the man who took an air-cushion with him to the Tribunal and claimed, and to everyone's surprise secured, absolute exemption. It was wonderful how that extraordinary machinery worked: the goats as often as not got through the gate and the sheep were incarcerated. Shortly afterwards Wake seems to have resigned his fellowship and about the same time his membership of the Fabian Society. In 1918 he unsuccessfully contested one of the Glasgow divisions as a member of the extreme Left of the Labour Party. Since then, after a brief flirtation with Communism, he has been shifting more and more to the Right, until now, I gather, he is looked upon with suspicion by the Party as one who will rat to the Liberals as soon as their ship becomes a little more seaworthy. Obviously, Mr. Wake is a careerist, but no ordinary one. Friends of mine who have read his books speak of his extraordinary ability. He is supposed to have made a small fortune by gambling on the foreign exchanges."

"Where does he live?" asked Jim.

"With his mother and two sisters in Essex—the Old Malt House, Shepherd's Colne. He does a certain amount of lecturing and journalistic work and has recently joined the Board of the European Investment Corporation, where, I imagine, his knowledge will be particularly useful."

"Have you any ideas, sir, about the next steps we ought to take?" asked Jim.

"None of any value," said Sir Richard. "Frankly, I see little hope of getting hold of the incriminating letter. Wake has probably lodged it at his bankers or at a safe deposit. On the other hand it may possibly be in his house. A letter is the easiest thing to hide safely, the most difficult thing to find. You remember Poe's story of how the Paris police turned a house upside down in search of a letter which all the time was in a conspicuous place under their very noses?"

"Then you think that I ought to renew my acquaintance with Wake on the off chance of discovering it?" asked Jim.

"It seems the only thing to do," Sir Richard answered, "though I admit the chances of success are small. What excuse can we find for your visiting Shepherd's Colne?"

"A walking tour through Essex," said Diana, "with the object of studying the local churches."

"Do I look as if I was interested in local churches, Miss Conyers?" asked Jim, with a smile, "and am I the sort of enthusiast who would walk through Essex? No, I am afraid

Wake would catch me out as soon as I began to speak about ecclesiastical architecture. He's sure to be an authority on the subject. But how would this do? My cousin is on the look-out for a week-end cottage within easy distance of London. I could take a bicycle and a rucksack and wander round, hear by accident that Wake was living at the Old Malt House, and call to renew our acquaintance and get any information he can give me about likely properties."

It seemed to be as good a plan as any. There were one or two details still to decide. Sir Richard promised that he would keep Jim informed of any further developments. He would write, too, to Mr. Digby at Gaunt Lodge.

"Good night, Dr. Pickering," he said, as he shook hands. "I'm afraid it's almost useless and that we shall be unable to prevent Wake from springing his mine, in which case your reminiscences will make interesting reading for a future generation."

Jim, as he walked back to his rooms in Bloomsbury, did not feel that he was embarking upon a forlorn hope. If he found the letter at Shepherd's Colne, well and good. But even if he did not, there were other things which he might find. Supposing he could prove that Petch did not commit suicide but was murdered by Wake, or even if Wake could be shown to be guilty of manslaughter, they could move from the defensive to the offensive. Some people perhaps might say that it was meeting blackmail with blackmail. It would be well in any case to help Sir Richard out of it. But he was forgetting his uncle. A great deal, perhaps everything, might depend on the clues he picked up in Yorkshire. Surely between them they ought to be able to upset the schemes of Mr. Badman.

XIV
Shepherd's Colne

Next morning Jim stepped out of the train at Colchester, a bulging rucksack slung across his shoulders. From the luggage-van he rescued his bicycle. It was nearly a year since he had last ridden the machine and he took the opportunity of an early lunch to leave it at a garage for a hasty overhaul. He had already provided himself with a map, and with it stretched out before him on the table he planned his route. It was his intention to arrive at Shepherd's Colne early in the evening. The search for a week-end cottage was the nominal reason for his being in that district, and he told himself that the best and safest plan would be to play his part in earnest, if Wake's suspicions were not to be aroused.

By half-past one he was on the Mersea road free-wheeling before a following wind. It was indeed a glorious afternoon, and in the lanes and by-roads that he followed there were no motors to break the silence of the countryside, only an occasional carrier's cart or slow trotting farmer's gig.

When at five o'clock he dismounted from his machine

outside the post-office in the main street of Shepherd's Colne, he had passed through a dozen villages which were no longer names on a map but casual acquaintances which time might fashion into friends. By the postmistress he was directed to Mrs. Pingo's, who, she informed him, occasionally did for young men. Would he be staying long in Shepherd's Colne? She was afraid he would find it terribly quiet. But then some people seemed to like the quiet. There was that artist that Mrs. Pingo had had last autumn. He had been painting a picture for the Royal Academy. Perhaps the gentleman remembered it. It was called "When Evening Smiles," and the old man driving home the cows was Jacob Basset, Mrs. Pingo's brother-in-law, though his beard was really whiter than that.

Jim found at Mrs. Pingo's exactly the accommodation he required, and in his landlady a gossip who needed no prompting. As he did justice to her bacon and eggs, she revealed to him the little world of Shepherd's Colne. Sir Crofton Villiers was away big game-shooting in Africa. Lady Villiers had started a Women's Institute and she and the vicar's wife taught fancy-work to the women that came; but there weren't many, as Shepherd's Colne, being mostly Nonconformist, didn't hold with Lady Villiers reading plays while they worked. Mrs. Topham at the Crossways, who bred Alsatians, had quarrelled with the vicar, whose gardener had been bitten by one of her pups, and she had refused to allow Miss Jones, her kennel-maid, to teach in the Sunday School. One of the Miss Wakes at the Old Malt House had been asked to take her place, but it seemed she didn't hold with religion and her mother was a Roman Catholic.

"Is it Mr. Olaf Wake who lives at the Old Malt House?" asked Jim. "I met him only a week ago in Yorkshire."

"And a fine spoken gentleman he is," said Mrs. Pingo. "He came here in the spring. It's wonderful the improvements he's made to the place: telephone and electric light and I don't know what. He's what I call a hasset to Shepherd's Colne. The pity is that we don't see more of him."

From Mrs. Pingo Jim found out that the Old Malt House was about three-quarters of a mile from the village, and as soon as he had finished his after-tea pipe he set out to renew acquaintance with Mr. Olaf Wake.

"If you've got the time," said Mrs. Pingo, "you should look into the church on your way. They've been repairing it all summer and the scaffolding's still round the steeple. They'll have finished that in a day or two, though, and then they'll have made a proper job of it, though in my opinion the war memorial by rights should have been on the village green."

The Old Malt House was approached by a narrow lane leading off from the high road. It was a tall red-brick building of the period of Queen Anne, flanked on one side by a walled garden that sloped gently to a creek that flowed into the Blackwater. The tide was out and a moored punt lay stranded in the mud.

Jim walked up the drive and rang the bell. It was answered by a neat little waiting-maid. Mr. Wake was at home and Jim was shown into the library. Wake was seated at a desk by the window, busy writing.

"Dr. Pickering," he said, as he rose to greet him, "this is an unexpected pleasure! It's a long cry from Gaunt Lodge to the Old Malt House. I heard from our friend Stillwinter only this morning. He told me that you had gone up to town and that he had persuaded Mr. Digby to be his guest. I wish I could have seen more of your uncle. He struck me as a most remarkable man. But what made you leave Yorkshire moors for Essex backwaters in July?"

"House-hunting," said Jim. "My uncle and I had planned to make Keldstone the centre for a walking tour, and then, as luck would have it, he sprained his ankle a few days ago. So I've taken the opportunity of working off an old commission from my cousin, who wants to find a week-end cottage within easy reach of London. She is by way of being an artist and Essex has always appealed to her. My business is to reassure her about drains and water. I cycled down from Colchester this afternoon, liked the look of Shepherd's Colne, and then found to my surprise from my gossip of a landlady that you lived here."

"You couldn't do better than make Shepherd's Colne your centre for a few days," said Wake. "I wish it had been possible for us to put you up here, but we are expecting guests to-morrow and it would be no kindness to get you to upset your arrangements for one night. But let me introduce you to my mother and sisters. I expect we shall find them in the garden."

At one corner of the walled garden was an old-fashioned summer-house. There they found Mrs. Wake and the younger of her two daughters, Adela. Miss Wake, it appeared, had been summoned to a committee that was to appoint a new district nurse.

"My sister," said Wake with a smile, "was trained as a

nurse during the war, and her chief quarrel with Shepherd's Colne is that the place is far too healthy and gives no scope for her advice and skill."

Jim was bidden by Mrs. Wake to take the seat on her right and not to drop his voice in conversation, as she was a little deaf. He found her a charming old lady, with very distinct views of her own. She was interested to hear that he knew the Stillwinters. "He was an old flame of mine," she said, "but I told him that if we married, I really couldn't have him wandering about Arabia and Thibet and that he would have to settle down. If a woman's place is the home, her husband's is certainly not the desert. He used to speak very tragically about his work, the nature of which I could never quite understand, and we eventually parted on excellent terms. I am afraid his sister spoils him; she had far too great a capacity for hero worship."

While Mrs. Wake talked, Jim was busy studying her daughter. How far, he wondered, was she in her brother's confidence? She had at all events strength of character, if none of her mother's charm. The mouth looked as if it could keep a secret, and the dark eyes beneath their half-lowered lids seemed quite capable of discovering one.

"By the way," said Wake, "you must have left Keldstone about the same time as Miss Conyers. Stillwinter told me that she had gone up to town. He made out that he was quite hurt that she had not called to say good-bye."

Was he trying to sound him, Jim wondered? How much did the man know of his connection with Diana and her affairs? He decided that deception might be more risky than the truth.

"As a matter of fact," he said, "we travelled up together. She said something about Lady Mottram not being well and of her having to take her place at a number of functions. What a ghastly life it must be, opening bazaars and institutions and being presented with bouquets by chairmen's daughters and golden keys that are no use to anyone, not even a burglar!"

"Perfectly futile," Wake agreed, "especially for a girl like Miss Conyers, who, from what I have seen of her, strikes me as being exceptionally well endowed with intelligence for the daughter of a Cabinet Minister. Have you ever met Sir Richard Mottram?"

For a moment Jim hesitated. This time he determined that he would lie.

"No," he said; "at least only at a political meeting a year ago, when he talked a lot of rot about the red peril in our midst and kicking out Bolshevist emissaries."

Wake smiled. "It's rot, of course," he said, "but Mottram has the gift of interpreting the people's pulse and what I suppose you doctors would call prognosis. He's an able politician, but from what I hear I shouldn't be surprised if the strain of the last few years won't prove too much for him. You need an iron constitution nowadays if you are to play a part in public life. But what do you say to a game of croquet? When played as it should be played, it really makes an excellent game. Adela, you had better take mother in; it's time she had her rest. And tell Sophie to bring out a pair of my shoes for Dr. Pickering."

The old lady got up from her seat and held out her hand. For the first time Jim noticed how old and frail she was.

"Good-bye, Dr. Pickering," she said. "I am so glad we have met. And you must come and pay your respects to me to-morrow when you have any time left over from house-hunting."

The game of croquet, from Jim's point of view, was not a success. It was new to him, for this was not the light-hearted battering of splintered balls through misshapen hoops that he had known as a boy, and though Wake, with infinite patience, instructed him in the theory of its strategy, he had all the time the feeling that he was being watched, weighed up. He had come to the Old Malt House to find out more about Olaf Wake; when at last the game was finished and the balls, carefully wiped by Wake, replaced in their box, he was left with the weary conviction that Olaf Wake had somehow managed to find out a great deal about him.

"We seem to have avoided the subject of desirable week-end cottages," said Wake with a smile, "but you mustn't forget your promise to my mother to look her up to-morrow and we can discuss the matter then."

As he walked back to his lodgings, Jim became more than ever convinced that he was making a mess of things. Time was precious and what had he to show for the labours of the day? He had found out nothing, except that he liked old Mrs. Wake and distrusted her daughter. He had done nothing, except to establish more or less friendly relations with people who were probably quite aware of his motives and who, as likely as not, were chuckling quietly over his impotence.

By the light of a lamp that smoked abominably he wrote a letter to Mr. Digby. He would have liked to write to Diana too, but he had nothing to report and she was probably expecting big things from him. He turned for solace to Mrs. Pingo's library, a dozen books which, thanks to two bound volumes of the *Sunday at Home* at each end of the row, presented a united front on the bottom shelf of the dresser. But *Robinson Crusoe* was among them and with *Robinson Crusoe* he sat up until the clock in the kitchen struck ten. He had just risen to close the window before he went to bed, when Mrs. Pingo opened the door hurriedly.

"Oh, if you please, sir," she said, "they've just sent round from the post-office with a telephone message from the Old Malt House. Mrs. Wake has been took bad suddenly with her heart and they would be very glad if you could come as soon as you can. Dr. M'Kinnon has been called away to a case and they can't get on to him."

"All right," said Jim. "I suppose you haven't such a thing as a bicycle lamp?"

"Indeed I haven't, sir, but Joe Mullet will be down at the other end of the village for closing time at the 'Crown and Anchor.' There's no fear that he will bother you."

With the doctor's feeling of resentment against the world in general at receiving another man's night call and that, too, on a holiday, Jim mounted his machine. The night was dark, but sufficiently clear for him to distinguish the white ribbon of the road. He had almost reached the turning to the left that led to the Old Malt House when he heard the sound of a car behind him. Suddenly the headlights were switched on and in the unexpected glare his machine swerved. He was conscious of a terrific blow on the head, the night was lit by a thousand stars, and then darkness engulfed him.

XV
The Flag in the Mirror

A SPLITTING HEADACHE—AND, WHEN HE LIFTED HIS hand to his brow, there were bandages round his head. Light streamed into the room past the edges of a lowered blind. Was it morning or evening? He was too tired to think. But he was too tired to sleep, too; aching limbs dragged him from the world of oblivion he fain would seek into unwelcome consciousness of his surroundings. He was lying in bed, but the bed, despite its clean linen sheets, had an unfamiliar feel about it. The mattress was surely unusually hard, and what on earth was that contraption at the foot of the bed with cords and pulleys? Then in a flash he realised what was the matter. His left leg was fractured and they had put on extension to bring the two ends of the broken bone into line. It had been a nasty smash. What about the other leg, he wondered? He tried to move it, only to find that it was firmly encased in a box splint.

"Well, I'm blessed!" said Jim.

"You are feeling better, then," said a voice, and for the

first time he noticed that he was not alone in the room. A nurse had risen from a low chair in a recess by the window.

"You have had a long sleep," she said. "I'm going to leave you now to warm some milk; then after a wash you'll feel better still."

"Where am I?" asked Jim, "and what exactly is the matter with me?"

"You are in the cottage hospital at Partington," said the nurse, "with a fractured femur and ankle, and you've had concussion, too. But don't you worry; the worst is over and Dr. Kent thinks you should do very well."

"Tell me what the time is and then I'll be quiet."

The nurse looked at her watch. "It's nearly two o'clock. Dr. Kent will be here after tea. And now I must see about your milk."

Two o'clock and half the day still before him! And after that weeks of enforced idleness with perhaps a game leg at the end of it and Sir Richard, all unknowing, pinning his hopes on a broken man!

The room was very still. Somewhere behind the lowered blind a fly was droning, futile, monotonous; for both of them the room was a prison. But it was certainly clean and airy; large, too, for a cottage hospital, and the nurse seemed efficient. His opinion of her skill increased during the afternoon. She had a gift of arranging pillows, of quiet movement, and of silence.

Dr. Kent was late in his visit, and before he came Jim had slept. Kent was a man of about forty; he had red hair and a short, pointed beard. With a cigar and a quarter-deck he might have passed for Captain Kettle. The hand with which he felt Jim's pulse was the broad, capable hand of a surgeon.

"Temperature subnormal, I see," he said. "Now let's have a look at the pupils. I'm not going to disturb the dressings. It was a nasty scalp wound, but clean."

"Well, doctor," he went on when his examination was finished, "it seems a bit cynical to congratulate you, but you've had a lucky escape. The fractures are simple ones, and I'll stake my reputation," he added with a smile, "that there will be no shortening or deformity of any kind. But what were you doing to get smashed up like that?"

"Like a fool I was cycling without a lamp and was blinded by the headlights of an overtaking motor. I suppose the cads drove on and left me in the ditch."

"On the contrary they brought you here. They showed due concern and the owner left his name and address. He's a big rose-grower somewhere on the other side of Colchester."

"But ah! he left the thorn with me," said Jim with a smile, "the confounded crimson rambler. Anyhow, I've you to thank for what looks like an excellent bit of splicing."

"Don't mention it, my dear fellow. It was all in the day's work, or rather the night's. But you have talked quite long enough. I'll look in again some time to-morrow; and in the meantime you can put implicit confidence in Nurse Peregrine. But I was forgetting—what about letting your people know?"

Jim thought for a moment.

"I don't think there's any need to alarm them," he said at last. "I'll get the nurse to send a wire in the morning, or write."

"It might perhaps be better to write," the doctor answered, "unless you want them to come down here at once. A telegram has a nasty way of reproducing all the alarm and terror of the actual accident. You break the news with all the suddenness with which you break the limb."

Jim awoke the next morning with his headache gone and a craving for bacon and eggs. He was in a mood of healthy disgruntlement, which, however, was incapable of ruffling the serenity of Nurse Peregrine. With difficulty he wrote two pencilled notes to Mr. Digby and Diana Conyers, explaining the reason for his enforced inactivity. He spoke lightly of his injuries, for the last thing he wished was to bring his uncle hurrying down from Yorkshire, when everything depended now upon him.

At eleven o'clock Nurse Peregrine to his surprise announced a visitor. It was Adela Wake, no longer cynical, but slightly effusive.

"We were most awfully sorry to hear about your accident," she said, "and in a way I'm afraid we are responsible for it. Mother didn't want us to telephone; she insisted that there was nothing really the matter with her; but my sister Bridget, who knows about these things, was rather alarmed. I do hope you have got through the worst. It must be simply awful having to lie up like that. My brother would have called, but he had to go up to London on urgent business. He told me to say that if there is anything you want, anything he can do for you, you mustn't hesitate to let him know. Mother sent these grapes and flowers with her love, and we thought you might be glad of some novels to read."

"It's most kind of her and you," said Jim, as soon as Miss Wake had paused for breath. "I really couldn't be better looked after than I am here. As far as I can find out, I'm about the only patient about the place, and Nurse Peregrine seems glad that I've given her something to do."

"You like her?"

"She knows her job and that is all that one requires of a nurse. But tell me more about Dr. Kent."

"Oh, Dr. Kent! He's an eccentric in his way but a first-rate surgeon. I believe he's a specialist in ortho—what is the word?—orthoaedics. He's been frightfully keen on getting this cottage hospital started and in running it on model lines, which means overriding his committee and getting it hopelessly into debt."

Jim turned the conversation on to her brother and his activities, but Miss Wake was not communicative, and after ten minutes she rose to say good-bye.

"Are you motoring?" he asked.

"No, I came on my cycle; it's not far and I'm glad of the exercise. You must let us know when you run out of books."

When Dr. Kent came in the late afternoon, he did not stay long, but he brought with him a copy of the *Times*, which Jim found more than usually interesting. Lord Whincastle, the Foreign Secretary, was critically ill; there were rumours of his resignation. Events were stirring in the political world and the prophets were busy. In the city there had been a big sensation in the unexpected failure of the Anglo-Italian Banking Corporation. Jim knew little about politics and less about international finance, and he wished Mr. Digby were there to explain in his shrewd way the intricacies of their connection. In any case Sir Richard Mottram would be in the thick of things. It was his hour, his opportunity, and Jim knew enough of him to be sure that he would seize it.

When he awoke next morning, he was reminded of the fact that it was Sunday by the sound of church bells. There would be no paper that day. He had finished his novels and there was nothing to do. Nurse Peregrine, despite her efficiency, was not quite the perfect nurse, not at least for convalescence. She was too silent, and if she had any sense of humour she did not bring it with her when she came on duty. Jim suggested that his bed should be moved to the window; he was tired of seeing nothing but blue sky behind white curtains and wanted a middle distance. Nurse Peregrine, however, pointed out that there were no castors on the bed, that he was no light weight, and that she was short-handed. She did not appear to be in a very helpful mood. Her duties finished, he was left to his own resources.

There came a tap at the door, and before he had time to reply it was opened and a maid looked into the room.

"Oh, I beg your pardon, sir," she said; "is Miss Adela here?"

The silliness of the question made him laugh.

"Miss Adela," he said, "was here yesterday. But now that you are here, you can do me a service and move the dressing-table and the mirror, so that I can at least see some reflection of the outside world. That's it; just a trifle more to the left. I'm very much obliged."

There was something almost furtive in the way the girl closed the door.

"I hope she's not going to get it in the neck from the powers that be," thought Jim. "It looks as if I were in for another visit from Miss Adela."

But if the maid had infringed hospital discipline, her

delinquency had not passed unnoticed. He heard voices in the corridor and could distinguish Nurse Peregrine's raised in shrill expostulation. There came the sound of a muffled blow, and sobs.

"You shan't hit me, miss," he heard, "you shan't hit me!"

"The unholy brute!" he exclaimed. "What the dickens has the girl done wrong?" And who the dickens was the girl? Surely now he came to think of it, he had seen her before. In a flash he remembered. It was she who had opened the door to him when he had called on the Wakes last Thursday evening. But what was she doing here at Partington in the same neat uniform? And why in the name of all that was inexplicable should she call Nurse Peregrine miss? Was the hospital short-staffed and had she been loaned by the Wakes as a guilt offering or, more likely, as a thank offering? It seemed unlikely but he could think of no other reason that would account for her presence.

Idly his eyes made the familiar tour of the room that was his prison, to be arrested by the mirror, or rather the reflection in the mirror. There was not much to see: the tops of trees, and in the gap framed by their branches a church steeple surrounded by scaffolding. The weather-vane glistened in the sunshine and above it, fixed at a perilous angle, fluttered a Union Jack.

XVI
Mr. Digby Makes Discoveries

AFTER SAYING GOOD-BYE TO JIM AND DIANA ON THE platform of Keldstone station, Mr. Digby, leaning heavily upon his stick, made his way slowly back to Daniel Lavender's and set about the business of packing, a solemn ritual, in which all unseemly haste was banished. He placed two solid cowhide suit-cases that had seen long service, on two chairs by the bed. Then, after spreading sheets of newspaper over the counterpane, he proceeded to empty on them the contents of all his drawers, drew up a third chair, and sat down on it to ponder over a plan of campaign.

His first step was to place his razor, strop, sponge-bag, and Bible safely at the bottom of one of the suit-cases. Experience had taught him that they were the things which he usually left behind. Then, after the fashion of Noah, he mustered his belongings in pairs, each according to its kind, creeping things (slippers), two-legged creatures (pants), two-limbed garments (shirts and vests), linen and wool, clean and unclean, each according to its kind, entered his leathern ark. Shem, Ham, and Japhet, represented by carefully folded suits, followed, and the door was shut and locked, only to be opened again in a moment to admit of the entrance of the dove, Mr. Digby's collar-box, which he had placed underneath his candlestick the night before when he was reading in bed. At last the work was finished and Mr. Noah was ready to set out for Ararat.

The Stillwinters gave him the warmest of welcomes. It was evident from the first that Miss Stillwinter was determined to treat him as an invalid.

"You'll probably sprain your other ankle trying to escape from her cosseting," said Stillwinter, "and then you will be absolutely in her power and she perfectly happy. We have had one serious dispute about you already this morning, with the result that no room is prepared for you. Anne declared that you ought to sleep on the ground floor in order to avoid the necessity of climbing the stairs. I was equally emphatic that you would prefer the room that Wake had. If your ankle is nearly well, Digby, stand by me, there's a good fellow. Prestige is everything in a house like this, and Anne has a most annoying habit of thinking that she knows exactly what people want far better than they do themselves. I believe she calls it feminine intuition, and that is what we bachelors have been trying to escape from all our lives."

"I know, I know," said Mr. Digby. "My niece is just the same; it's most exasperating. I shall be perfectly happy in Wake's old room."

As he lay in bed that night, Mr. Digby reviewed the happenings of the day with mingled feelings. He liked his surroundings, he liked his hosts; he did not indeed dislike the knowledge that Miss Stillwinter was prepared to fuss over him at the slightest provocation. But he was making little, if any, progress in his search for clues. He placed his hand on the switch at the side of the bed, turned on the electric light, and once again glanced through the closely written pages of his pocket diary in an attempt to reconstruct the events of the last eight days. He began by putting himself in the place of Petch. He was almost certain that it was Petch who had called that night at Daniel Lavender's and whose visit he had interrupted. Obviously he had come for the book and its contents. When next day he had read the notice in the shop that announced the loss of the copy of *Mr. Badman*, he would at once think that someone had forestalled him. Granted that Petch knew that Offord and Wake were after the book—and surely it was not an improbable supposition—he would next turn his attention to them. Mr. Digby pictured him searching Worpleswick Vicarage from cellar to garret. As Offord's servant he would have every opportunity of discovering the volume, had Offord taken it, and not discovering it, he would naturally leap to the conclusion that somehow or other it had come into Wake's possession. Petch wanted it, he imagined, to ruin the man whose son had ruined his daughter. Wake and Offord were no friends of Sir Richard, but Petch did not trust them; Sir Richard might buy them off and maintain the honour of his house.

So far, so good, thought Mr. Digby. But what next? Petch would look for the book at Gaunt Lodge, in Wake's bedroom, in the room that he, Mr. Digby, was occupying now. It would be easy enough to get into the house, a broken window and…surely there had been some talk about a broken window! He remembered now. On the Thursday morning, the day of the discovery of the body, Wake had gone into Keldstone to get a plumber. He had thrown a stone at a stray cat, had missed the cat and smashed the glass, and Stillwinter had chuckled to find that there was at least one thing which his guest could not do supremely well. Petch had broken the window and Wake was only anxious that attention should not be called to it.

And now, said Mr. Digby to himself, Petch is inside the house, creeping along the passages on tiptoe in his search for the right room. Wake's boots, left outside the door, would be enough to give him the tip. Slowly he turns the handle of the door and makes out the figure of Wake, asleep in my bed. Silently he proceeds with his search; but Wake is aroused and switches on the light. Then he either fires straight away—what an uncomfortable and dangerous practice it must be to sleep with a loaded revolver underneath one's pillow!—or there is a demand for explanations and a quarrel. In any case there is murder done, shooting at very close quarters—Mr. Digby glanced round the room and wished that the bedside light were a little brighter—and Wake is left with the problem of disposing of the body. From the nature of the wound he sees that it is not incompatible with suicide, but Petch cannot be left there.

Mr. Digby, who had been more than pleased at his reconstruction of the crime, was brought up short. He had to get the body on to the moor; but the footprints, and very clear footprints they were, too, were those of Petch. Had the fatal quarrel taken place by the peat stacks? Wake might have thought of some plausible reason for giving a rendezvous there with the dead man, and shot him from the shelter of the thick heather. Yet Mr. Digby was loath to give up his original theory, and with a flash he realised that there was no reason why he should give it up. Wake had taken off the dead man's boots, put them on, and carried the body to a spot on the moor where the soft tell-tale peat ended and the rough ling, which would show no footprints, began. And he had carried the body—Mr. Digby's brain was working quickly now—in a rug or fur-lined overcoat. That would account for the hairs that Jim had discovered. They were present not only on the dead man's clothes but on his socks underneath his boots, which Wake had put on again before he finally left the body, half-recumbent, behind the peat stack.

It was with difficulty that Mr. Digby composed his mind for sleep, and when at last his head lay quiet on the pillow, it was into no peaceful slumber that he fell. In his dreams he was wandering in the moonlight over cold moors, searching for a lost Mongolian goat, while twelve Chinamen, armed with revolvers, followed stealthily in his tracks, urged on by Dr. Jacobs, who wore a sprig of shamrock in the buttonhole of his frock-coat.

"You have slept well, I hope, Mr. Digby," Miss Stillwinter asked next morning at breakfast.

"Of course, with an easy conscience like his and a comfortable bank balance, he has slept well in a bed shut in by four walls and with only six inches of open window."

"Eight," corrected Mr. Digby, "quite eight, when it's as still as last night."

"Pshaw, Digby, you ought to be ashamed of yourself. I

suppose you had a hot bottle, too. At your age you ought to be hardening yourself off, as my gardener would say, ready for bedding out. But seriously, why not try sleeping in the open air? I have any number of sleeping-bags I can lend you. All I do is to take out my bag and a ground sheet, choose a patch of springy heather for mattress, and there's my encampment. If there is a cold wind, I don't disdain a night cap. Anne knits them for me. I am sure she would be delighted to knit one for you. Nobody disturbs me and I disturb no one, now that the gamekeeper has got used to my night wanderings. What do you say about it?"

Mr. Digby took another slice of toast and slowly proceeded to butter it. He thought with affectionate regret of his own feather bed in Bradborough. He glanced appealingly at Miss Stillwinter.

"Philip," said that lady, "you are perfectly absurd. It was all very well for you to try and persuade Mr. Wake to share your bivouac, but what is the use of your having wandered about in Arabia, if you have learned no more of the duties of hospitality than to offer Mr. Digby muscular rheumatism, lumbago, and sciatica in the guise of a bed?"

"In Arabia," began Stillwinter, "the position of woman—"

"Must be very dreadful, I am sure, especially where there are no oases. Mr. Digby stays where he is. After breakfast you can show him your sleeping-bags and he can judge for himself."

With a sigh Stillwinter acknowledged defeat, but as soon as the meal was over, his spirits rose as he led the way to the lumber-room, where his old campaigning kit was stored. Mr. Digby was in a state of suppressed excitement.

Sleeping-bags! It was in a hair-lined sleeping-bag that Wake had removed the body.

"There they are," said Stillwinter, "in that pile in the corner. I use a Jaeger one nowadays, which I keep in the study. They've all seen hard wear and all are in good preservation. All that is wanted is a little foresight. Once a month the housemaid turns them inside out and leaves them for an hour or two to air in the sun. Then she sprinkles them with cedar chips."

"Cedar chips!" exclaimed Mr. Digby.

"Yes, they are far the best preservative against moths, if you wish to avoid the smell of chemicals. And the result is that if six friends were to call and all the beds were occupied, I could give them each an excellent shakedown... The only trouble is," he added, "that the six friends don't call."

Mr. Digby was busy examining the sleeping-bags.

"Tell me," he said, "have you by any chance one that is lined with goat-skin?"

"Yes, the one I used in Thibet in '95. Mongolian goat, beautifully warm! I'll find it for you in a minute... That's queer," he added, as he went through the pile. "I could have sworn it was here. I distinctly remember seeing it ten days ago when I was wasting my eloquence to no purpose on Wake. I wonder what can have become of it. It surely can't be due to a second outbreak of spring cleaning. We got through ours, I thought, unusually successfully and Anne does not often have a relapse. I've explained to her more than once that she mustn't have them."

"Do you think Wake repented of his decision not to sleep out?" asked Mr. Digby, "and perhaps later borrowed the bag, which he forgot to replace?"

"No, I don't," Stillwinter replied. "Wake is not the sort of man to change his mind and he is methodical to a fault. However, I suppose the thing will turn up some day."

Mr. Digby was less sure, because, as Stillwinter had said, Wake was methodical in his habits and would realise the importance of covering his tracks. But none the less he determined that he would find that sleeping-bag and that it should figure among his exhibits along with the hairs and cedar chips. Miss Stillwinter, a housemaid, the gardener, and the gardener's boy were enlisted in a search that extended from attic to potting-shed, and when it proved fruitless, Mr. Digby, evading the vigilance of his hostess with difficulty, slipped out of the house unobserved to the peat stacks, where he thought it possible that Wake might have concealed it. Half of the stacks, however, had been carted away, and his examination of the remainder proved fruitless.

But he was not dissatisfied with his day's work, and at dinner that evening Stillwinter let slip a piece of information which looked as if it might well prove to be the strongest link in the chain of evidence which was to fetter the activities of Olaf Wake.

"I did that young man an injustice, it seems," he said. "'Afterwards he repented and went'; in other words he did sleep out on Wednesday night. I thought at the time that sooner or later my arguments would be bound to carry weight, and I can quite understand his not saying anything about it. It's always dangerous to admit that you are in the wrong."

"And how did you find that out, Philip?" asked his sister.

"I met young Bryden, the keeper, this afternoon, taking

a busman's holiday. Your young nephew, Digby, rushed him over to Maltwick last week in his car for a sudden operation. It seems, though, that Bryden preferred to wait and see, and to everyone's surprise the offending organ responded to the trust which he put in it. Wild nature was won by kindness and the surgeons were bilked. We had some talk together and he mentioned how he had seen me leave the house on Wednesday night between twelve and one, humping my sleeping-bag and the rest of the paraphernalia on my back. I explained how at that hour I was fast asleep in the heather, but that this was a youthful convert to my faith and practice."

"Jim," said Mr. Digby, after a pause, "will be interested in hearing of the man's recovery. I know he took a very serious view of the case. I should rather like to look him up to-morrow and have a talk with him."

"But it was too bad of Wake," added Stillwinter, "to treat my property in such a casual fashion. I suppose when the shower came on at four that morning, he took to his heels and ran, meaning to retrieve the sleeping-bag later in the day. I always distrusted political economists. They are theoretical, essentially theoretical!"

XVII
All Among the Heather

FRIDAY'S POST BROUGHT MR. DIGBY THE LETTER from Sir Richard Mottram in which he learnt for the first time of Wake's threat and Jim's journey down into Essex. He wrote a brief acknowledgment, stating that he had been far more successful than he had hoped, and to Jim began a long letter in which he gave a detailed account of his discoveries. He asked Jim to find out, if possible, the size of Wake's boots. He had already the shape of the impression of Petch's foot, and if his theory were to hold, Wake's foot would be about the same size, or smaller. But he was interrupted in his task by the arrival of a telegram, a disturbing telegram, from Jim.

"Am laid up here owing to motor smash. No cause for anxiety, but shall be confined to bed for some days. Do not come. Write at once to me, care of Pingo, Shepherd's Colne, Essex, full details of what you have found out, but say nothing to M. and don't inform

him or D. of my accident. Will keep you informed by telegram.

"PICKERING."

Mr. Digby was, of course, alarmed. He read and re-read the telegram. Jim said there was no cause for anxiety; on the other hand, he was laid up in bed for some days. There might be a good deal more behind that than appeared at first sight. And why should he keep Mr. Digby informed by telegram, unless he were prevented from writing? That seemed to point surely to something serious. Then, too, the telegram was needlessly long. Jim must have been badly shaken up not to see that he could have conveyed what he wished to say in two-thirds of the words. There was a superfluity of prepositions. But if Jim was the victim of a nasty motor smash, ought not he, Mr. Digby, to ignore his nephew's injunction to stay where he was and leave at once for Essex? What good purpose was there to be served by his staying on at Gaunt Lodge?

He remembered the conversation of the previous evening. He had still to interview the gamekeeper, whose evidence might prove to be all-important, and he had to discover, if possible, the whereabouts of the lost sleeping-bag. The only reason he could think of for Wake not having returned it was the presence of tell-tale blood-stains not easy to get rid of. No, his work was not finished. It was Friday. He would make arrangements for leaving the Stillwinters on Monday, unless in the meantime he heard to the contrary from Jim.

That afternoon, Mr. Digby, eluding the vigilance of Miss Stillwinter, made his way by easy stages to the keeper's cottage.

He found Bryden busy at work in the garden, earthing up his potatoes, and they were soon in friendly conversation.

"I'm right sorry for Dr. Pickering," said Bryden. "It will be a bitter disappointment to him. I know he wanted to have me opened up. But as I said to the doctor at Maltwick, it's risky work dealing with a man's innards, and though I know they wanted to see what was wrong inside, I thought I'd give a bottle of medicine another chance."

Mr. Digby had no difficulty in getting Bryden to tell him what he had seen on the night of Petch's murder. He was passing the lodge gates soon after twelve on his way home from the woods, when a man with a large bundle on his back came out of the house and went down the garden in the direction of the moor. It was too dark for him to distinguish the man's features, but he was about the same height as Mr. Stillwinter and he had at once assumed that it was he. Bryden, who was already feeling ill, had wakened his mother as soon as he got back home, and he remembered distinctly that the time was then one o'clock.

While the man was speaking, Mr. Digby was busy summing him up. He determined that he would trust him.

"It's like this," he said, "and you must understand that what I am telling you now is spoken in the strictest confidence. You remember poor Petch? Dr. Pickering and I believe it possible that he was the victim of foul play. There are many indications which point to the fact that quite unknown to Mr. Stillwinter he was shot in Gaunt Lodge and that the body was removed in a sleeping-bag and deposited by the peat stacks on the moor. That sleeping-bag is missing and I want your help in finding it."

"Then if you are right, sir, the man I saw was the murderer."

"Yes, and that is why, when Mr. Stillwinter told me last night of what you had seen, I came to you for fuller details. He knows nothing of my suspicions; I have no wish to cause him needless distress, and Miss Stillwinter, I know, would be very much alarmed."

"What exactly do you wish me to do, sir?" asked Bryden.

"I want you to come with me and I will point out the exact spot where Petch's body was found. Then I want you to use your imagination, to think of all the likely places where the man who killed him could have hidden the bag, some quarry, some bog, within easy access of the spot. He might, of course, have buried it."

Together the two men made their way on to the moor. At the peat stacks Mr. Digby left his companion with instructions to let him know if his search proved successful. There was nothing more for him to do and, leaning heavily on his stick, he walked back slowly to Gaunt Lodge. He had been gone longer than he had expected; the postman had already asked for the letters; and with annoyance he realised that his letter to Jim was only half written. But he was able to telephone a telegram to Keldstone, in which his affectionate sympathy was limited only by eighteen words.

In the meantime Bryden had not been idle. His first step was to examine, as Mr. Digby had done, the remaining stacks of peat, but it soon became clear to him that the object for which he was searching was not there. Then, with the peat stacks as a centre, he began to cast round in a spiral, keeping a careful look-out for any signs of disturbance of the ground. There were one or two patches of bog, green with sphagnum moss. These he sounded with his stick, but to no purpose. The weather for the last week had been dry. If the sleeping-bag had been hidden there, it was most unlikely that it could have been forced down more than three feet below the surface without obvious traces of disturbance. From bog he turned to rock. By the side of the rough track that led to the place where the body had been found there was an outcrop of rock, from which some large boulders had broken away. Carefully he examined the crevices between them; ferns, a broken glass bottle, the white bones of a sheep, but that was all.

Nothing daunted, Bryden took a new line and, crossing the ridge of the moor, made his way to a valley, thick with green bracken and dotted here and there with stunted alders, down which flowed a little beck. He followed up the course of the stream, until he came to a place where the valley turned. There was a straggling line of shooting-butts. Only a month before Bryden had repaired them in readiness for the twelfth. Carefully he examined each, again without result. Then retracing his steps to the peat stacks, he sat down and meditatively filled his pipe. Gaunt Lodge lay below him. A figure in white—it would be Miss Stillwinter—was walking in the rose garden. A man in a blue shirt—it would be Tom Wilkinson, the gardener—seemed to be gazing intently at a mass of rocks. His pipe finished, Bryden made his way slowly in the direction of Gaunt Lodge.

"Evening, Tom," he said, leaning against the garden fence.

"Evening, Bill. How's yourself?"

"Fair to middling; they didn't cut me up this time. Making a rock garden?"

"That's the idea. Come and have a look at it."

Bryden swung himself over the fence and sat down on a wheelbarrow.

"It must be slow work," he said. "How much have you done in a week?"

"Last Thursday I put the top on old Everest over there. It took three of us, working all morning with crow-bars, not to mention Mr. Wake, who lent a hand as well. And so you're all right again, Bill?"

"I've been told not to start work till Monday, but I'm thinking I may have a bit of a stroll round to-night. Old Tom Crake has got his eye on the pheasants in the long wood. Well, good-night, Tom!"

"Good-night, Bill!"

That evening about eleven o'clock the steady glow of a pipe might have been seen behind the potting-shed where Bryden was sitting, his rough-haired terrier at his feet. Presently he heard the sound of a door shutting; Mr. Stillwinter had left the house for the night to seek his bed among the heather. Bryden waited for five minutes and then, knocking out his pipe, walked over to the rock garden. He carried in his hand a long iron rod, part of a broken steel railing, and with this he began to poke about in the soft earth behind Mount Everest. Presently he gave a grunt of satisfaction and the terrier, pricking up his ears, began to scratch with his forepaws in the soil.

"Get him out, Bob! Out with him, lad!" said Bryden.

He hurried back to the potting-shed, returning a couple of minutes later with a spade, with which he enlarged the hole that the terrier had already made. It was not long before he came upon what he was looking for; it was longer before he removed all traces of his search. With the bundle under his arm and the terrier at his heels he made his way back to his cottage. On the stone flags outside the door he brushed away the earth. Then, taking it into the kitchen, he lit the lamp and carefully proceeded to examine his find. It was the sleeping-bag right enough and it looked as if Mr. Digby had not been far out in his guess; for there were dark stains on the hair that lined it, which even in the dim lamplight Bryden recognised as the stains of blood.

XVIII
Dr. Pickering
Feels His Feet

JIM CONTINUED TO GAZE AT THE REFLECTION IN THE mirror of the spire surrounded by its scaffolding and the flag that fluttered above the weather-vane. What was it that Mrs. Pingo had said about repairing the steeple at Shepherd's Colne? Slowly and painfully he was taking in the fact that he had been taken in; that he was not, as he had supposed, in the cottage hospital at Partington, but somewhere else. The neat little maid who had moved the mirror had as good as told him where.

Little by little he began to put the links in the chain of evidence together. He remembered how on the Thursday evening when he had first called, they had spoken of the elder Miss Wake, whom he had not seen, as being interested in nursing. Nurse Peregrine was explained. But who was Dr. Kent? The man was a doctor right enough; Jim had no doubts about that. But it was equally clear that he was an unscrupulous rogue, content to work hand and glove with the Wakes. What, he asked himself, was the motive of it all?

He tried to recall what had happened on the Thursday evening, when he had first set foot within the Old Malt House. They had suspected him probably from the first. They had found out that he had travelled up to London with Diana. But if they suspected him, it was more than probable that they would suspect Mr. Digby too, especially when they heard that he was staying with the Stillwinters. The warning letter to Sir Richard Mottram had been sent, in which he had been given ten days to make his decision. Jim could imagine that Wake would give a good deal to know what was passing in the enemy's camp.

And then he realised how simple a matter it all was. Wake was not afraid of him but of Mr. Digby and of what he might discover in the neighbourhood of Keldstone. He had probably wired to Mr. Digby in Jim's name to find out exactly what Mr. Digby had done and proposed to do. He could afford, too, to tell him half the truth, that Jim had been mixed up in a motor smash, an excellent reason for his not writing. His uncle's letters would be addressed to Mrs. Pingo's, where Wake would call for them. Wake would kill two birds with one stone. Watson—and Jim smiled grimly as he identified himself with the character—was safely laid by the heels and at the same time was being used as a decoy to draw out from Sherlock Holmes the secret of his plans. Watson doubtless could be used, too, as a hostage, if the worst came to the worst.

Devoutly he hoped that Mr. Digby had said nothing. If Wake or Kent had wired for information on Friday morning, that is, as soon as Jim was a prisoner, a letter in reply could hardly reach Shepherd's Colne before Sunday, and would be delivered first thing on Monday. But supposing Mr. Digby had *telegraphed* details of their counter-offensive against Wake? Surely he would not be so rash as to do that! His uncle's appreciation of the value of economy in telegrams would alone make him hesitate.

His thoughts were interrupted by the entrance of Nurse Peregrine with a glass of milk.

"Are there any letters for me?" he asked. "I ought to be hearing from my people."

"I'm afraid you will have to wait until to-morrow, doctor," she said; "there's no delivery on Sundays."

She was standing, as she spoke, by the dressing-table and Jim saw her push with her elbow the mirror. Once again he was gazing at blue sky. He asked if she expected a visit from Dr. Kent. Nurse Peregrine thought it was possible he might call in some time during the afternoon but she was not sure.

Once again he was left alone with his thoughts. How was he to get in touch with the world outside, with Mr. Digby and Sir Richard? Could he somehow get hold of the little housemaid and persuade her to send a telegram or letter? He turned over in his mind one plan after another, but all to no purpose. Miss Wake was already on her guard; it was not likely that there would be any more inadvertent trespassers into his bedroom. No, it was impossible to get a message through; but was it impossible for him to escape? His right ankle fractured, that alone ought not to stop him; but the other leg, the broken femur, that was an altogether different proposition.

Then suddenly there dawned upon his mind a possibility so novel, so unexpected, that it left him gasping. Were his limbs broken in that motor smash or had his leg, or rather his legs, been literally and figuratively pulled by Wake and Co.? If their purpose was to make him and keep him a prisoner without arousing his own or anyone else's suspicion, how better could it have been done than by confining him to bed, safely anchored by a very efficient bit of double splinting? Kent, with that sardonic humour that played about his mouth, would be exactly the man to appreciate the exquisite nature of the joke—he had promised that there would be no permanent shortening—while Wake would appreciate its value. Obviously he had been badly bruised—the pain alone told him that but what evidence was there of fracture beyond the presence of the splints?

Once the idea had entered his mind, it took complete possession of it. His theory could only be verified by removing the splints and bandages. That would be easy enough to do, but he would have to wait until night, when the coast would be clear. Then he would put matters to the test. Meanwhile he had the rest of the day in which to make his plans.

Even if his wild theory were correct, it would be by no means all plain sailing. His clothes had vanished; it would be necessary to do a little amateur burgling, necessary above all things to get to Mrs. Pingo's or to the Shepherd's Colne post-office at an early hour on Monday morning and either to collect any letters that were there or to make arrangements for their not being intercepted by Wake.

The long morning dragged on and the longer afternoon. Dr. Kent called after tea and dressed Jim's scalp wound.

"What about X-raying the fractures?" Jim asked.

"It should certainly be done," said Kent, "but the question

is when? As I told you before, I'm willing to stake my professional reputation on a satisfactory result, which the X-ray will confirm. One wants that confirmation, of course, if only for your peace of mind. But we can't very well move you at present. As soon as I think it can be done without risk, I'll arrange for a motor-ambulance to take you to wherever you want to go. But don't be in a hurry, Pickering. Possess your soul in patience and thank your lucky stars that things are no worse than they are."

Dr. Kent stayed for half an hour, talking. He could tell a story well and evidently had an eye for character. Despite himself, Jim could not at times refrain from laughing. At last he rose to go.

"There's nothing more I can do for you, doctor?" he asked.

"I should be grateful for a spot of dope to-night," said Jim. "I won't take it unless I really can't go to sleep, but I didn't get off until after three last night. I have a feeling that if it's there for me to take if I want it, and if I know that Nurse Peregrine won't disturb me before eight, I shall sleep like a top."

"Right you are, doctor, it shall be done. It would take a good deal to make you into a drug addict, my boy."

Nurse Peregrine had usually finished her duties well before ten, but to-night she was early and it was barely half-past nine when, after leaving his sleeping-draught on the chair by the bedside, she bade him good night.

Jim waited fifteen minutes, thirty minutes, in case of interruption. Then he began to act. There was an electric lamp by his bedside, but the light might call attention to the fact that he was awake. Later he would have to use it, but for the present he preferred to work in the dark. He tackled his right leg first. If he were wrong, if after all there were a fracture, it might be possible for him to rearrange the splint and bandages in such a way as to avoid the suspicion of having deliberately tampered with them.

The task was awkward but not difficult, and as it proceeded his spirits rose. The splint was free now and very gently he raised his right foot. The ankle was horribly stiff, there was no doubt about that, but when gingerly he attempted to flex and extend the joint, he found that there was nothing worse than stiffness. He put the foot on the floor, leaning heavily upon it. Yes, there was no fracture, that was certain; and he turned with renewed energy to the liberation of the other limb. This was not quite so easy a matter, for the removal of the adhesive strapping was a slow and tedious business, but at last it was free.

Jim placed the lamp on the floor, where its light would be less likely to be seen from outside, and sat on the side of the bed to complete the painful and humiliating process of self-examination. His left leg, like his right ankle, showed extensive bruisings. It was horribly stiff and he thought it possible that there might be a rupture of one of the ligaments of the knee; but the limb could support his weight. Again there was no fracture. As a precautionary measure he reapplied strapping and bandages to the knee and then with a sigh of satisfaction sat down in a chair. It was just after half-past ten.

What should be his next step? The whole night lay before him and he could well afford a few hours' sleep. But

Jim wanted a range of action wider than that given by the possession of a night-shirt and bed-jacket. There were no clothes in the chest of drawers. He did not even possess a dressing-gown. Reluctantly he made up his mind that it was too early to borrow from Wake's wardrobe and that he might as well sleep.

Long years ago he had schooled himself to wake at the required hour. It was three o'clock when he again got out of bed and quietly opened the door of his room. His room was at the back of the house on the third floor. Where was Wake's and Kent's? Or had they left the Old Malt House? In his bare feet he crept downstairs through the kitchen into the scullery. There, laid out all ready to be cleaned, he found two pairs of ladies' shoes and a pair of boots, that he recognised as Kent's. Wake, then, was away and Kent the only man he had to reckon with, apart from any men-servants there might be about the place. He unbolted and unlocked the scullery door, in case he should require an emergency exit, slipped on an overcoat that he found hanging in the hall, and made his way upstairs again. On the first floor there seemed to be four bedrooms. Three of them Jim assigned to Mrs. Wake and her daughters. The fourth he thought more likely to be Wake's than Kent's. But how could he tell which room was empty? Dare he open the door of each in turn to see? Jim determined that it would be too risky. Instead he went downstairs again, unlocked the front door and walked out on to the drive. In the dim light of early dawn he gazed up at the front of the Old Malt House and noticed that all the windows except two on the first floor rooms were open. They belonged evidently to the same room; the chances were all against it being occupied and there was a distinct probability that it would prove to be Wake's.

Jim was right. When he opened the door, his first glance told him that the room was empty. His first task was to close the shutters; his second to switch on the electric light. Then, losing no time, he proceeded to ransack the wardrobe. It was one of those pieces of furniture that he had always longed to possess, in which there was a place for everything and everything was in its place. In half an hour Jim, shaved and dressed, was ready to face the outside world. But he had not yet done with the Old Malt House. There was still the chance that he might discover, if not the all-important letter—that, indeed, he thought would be most unlikely—at least some document that might afford a clue. The bedroom told him nothing about Wake, except that he was extraordinarily tidy, fussily tidy. It was to the library that he turned with greater expectations.

He began his search with all the accumulated energy of three idle days, but at the end of two hours he gave up in despair. He had gone through desks and shelves, cupboards and drawers; he had turned out the waste-paper basket; he had even examined the blotting-paper with the help of a mirror in the best approved fashion of the detective of fiction; and all to no purpose. Disconsolate, he took up a Bradshaw and began to look up trains. The nearest station was Pent Bridge, about five miles away. There was a train at 6.10, another at 8.45. If he took the earlier of the two there would be no means of calling for his letters. No, the 8.45 was the one to aim at. He looked at his watch and found that it was nearly a quarter past five. There was plenty of time for him to make himself a cup of tea and to rake together a breakfast out of the remains of Sunday's supper. The food and hot drink together pulled him out of the slough of despond, half-mental, half-physical, into which he had fallen. With care he selected a hat from the stand in the hall and a strong ash plant that had seen good service. Then he let himself out of the house into the cool fresh air of the July morning.

Jim took his time over the walk to Shepherd's Colne. His left ankle was painful, his right leg horribly stiff. Soon after seven he called at Mrs. Pingo's. The good woman was already up and about and gave him a warm welcome.

"Well, Doctor," she said, "I was beginning to fear from all I heard that you were laid up for a long spell. I blame myself, that I do, for letting you ride off that night without your lamp. The roads aren't safe with these motors."

It was with difficulty that Jim could make her accept payment for his night's lodgings. He asked her if any letters had come for him while he was away.

"There was a telegram on Friday, which I sent up to the Old Malt House. They called to see if there were any letters for you regularly every day."

"In case any come," said Jim, "I want you to forward them at once to this address and to say nothing about it to Mr. Wake. He didn't want me to leave the Old Malt House, but I felt I couldn't trespass any longer on his hospitality. I shall very likely meet him again in London and will explain things then, but for the present I don't want him to know my address. You quite understand? And tell me, Mrs. Pingo, do you know a Dr. Kent, a tall man with a red beard, who practises round here?"

"There's only Dr. M'Kinnon," she answered, "and he's stout and clean-shaven. Perhaps you was thinking of Dr. Wiltshire, who was his local tenant last year, a nice spoken young man with spectacles. He hadn't a beard then, but I always said he'd be well advised to grow one. It sort of gives your patients confidence when you've got an open face."

From Mrs. Pingo Jim found out that the landlord of the "Crown and Anchor" was the owner of a Ford car. The man was willing enough to take him into Pent Bridge, and while he was filling up with petrol, Jim interviewed the postmistress. The mail had just come in. There was a fat envelope for him, addressed in Mr. Digby's writing. He filled up a form for the redirection of letters and wrote out a telegram to his uncle.

"Meet me at Bloomsbury address to-day, if possible. Till then ignore all wires, unless signed Jimbo. Have messed things badly at this end."

Jimbo was the nickname with which his uncle had christened him in the far-off days when he had spent delectable holidays in Bradborough, a secret name that would be safe from forgery. It was ten minutes past eight. The car was waiting for him outside. And Nurse Peregrine, he thought with a smile, would be busy arranging on a tray an appetising breakfast that never would be eaten.

XIX
Mr. Digby Takes the Lead

IT WAS HALF-PAST ELEVEN WHEN JIM GOT BACK TO HIS old quarters in Bloomsbury. The first thing he did was to telephone to Diana to find out when and where they could meet.

"I've lots to talk to you about," he said, "but it will take some time in the telling. I got a letter from my uncle this morning. He has got information which ought to give us the whip hand over Wake and Co. I bungled things badly down at Shepherd's Colne. Now where can we meet? Are you free this afternoon?"

"As a matter of fact," she said, "I was thinking of running over to Guildford in the two-seater. I'll call for you in half an hour and we'll lunch somewhere on the way. I'm longing to hear how you got on."

There was just time for a hot bath and a change, for a hurried note to Miss Wake, thanking her for her hospitality and for the clothes which he had borrowed and which he was returning. "Your brother's stick," he added in a postscript, "I am keeping for the present; I expect in the near future I shall have an opportunity of giving it him myself."

Diana was punctual.

"Why, Doctor Pickering!" she exclaimed, as they shook hands, "whatever have you been doing with yourself? And have you hurt your leg?"

"That's all right," he said, as he swung himself with difficulty into the seat beside her, "or at least it will be in a week's time. The long and short of it is that I've been playing the fool and got what I've deserved. Wait until we've got out of the traffic and I'll tell you the story. But keep your comments to the end and be prepared to judge with charity."

The car was a new one, a Morton Ashby, and Diana handled it well.

"When I last saw Wake," she said, "at the Stillwinters', I told him all about my latest purchase, and he was good enough to commend my choice, though he disapproved of the light-blue body as being too conspicuous. He held forth, I remember, on the advantages that a motorist enjoys by not attracting attention."

"And my story," said Jim, "is an excellent illustration of the point. I may as well get it over now. But first you shall hear the contents of my uncle's letter."

"Now you know everything," he said, when he had finished. "But don't pass verdict on me before we have lunched. No one can look for clemency from a hungry judge, and I know I'm ravenous."

Diana swung the car from the highroad into a lane.

"We'll lunch then at the first spot we find that is worthy of the occasion. I brought sandwiches with me. What about that patch of common away over there? If we can't have Yorkshire heather, we may as well make the most of what Surrey has to offer."

She drove the car along a rough track until it could go no farther. Then, leaving it, they made their way to a little group of firs that crowned a knoll.

"Well, Doctor Pickering," she said with a smile, "the verdict of the court can't wait. You leave this spot without a stain on your character. But seriously, I'm most awfully grateful for all you've done to help us. You deserved success, if anyone did. And you mustn't mind if on this occasion Wake outwitted you."

"Be good, dear Watson; let who will be clever. Yes, I know exactly what you mean. But all the same I sympathise with the typical small boy who has no particular desire to be good. It's only once in a blue moon that you get a man like my uncle, who combines the wisdom of the serpent and the innocence of the dove. But I've not heard yet how you have fared."

"To begin with," she said, "we've had a man shadowing Wake since Saturday, when my father had a long talk with the P.M. Wake is staying at the house of a Dr. Kemp in Hampstead, Cornelian Lodge. Kemp's sister, it seems, was engaged to the elder of Wake's brothers, the one who was shot by the Black and Tans. Kemp himself was at one time on the staff of an Irish Republican mission to the States. He is still supposed to be in control of large funds which were raised for the purposes of propaganda."

"I suppose he is Kent, my late medical attendant."

"He is described as middle-aged, tall, and handsome, with a pointed reddish beard. The Special Department at

Scotland Yard know quite a lot about him. I should think there can be no doubt that he and Wake are working together. What do you think our next step should be?"

"We must wait until my uncle arrives and then hold a council of war. If he caught the morning train from Keldstone, he should be at King's Cross soon after five. In the meantime let's forget about Mr. Badman. The day is too good for him to spoil."

They did not hurry over lunch. A soft wind, blowing from the common, brought with it the scent of gorse to mingle with the smell of the fir trees in whose shadow they lay. They talked of many things, of birds and books, of the ideal walking tour and the perfect caravan. Jim had great plans for a holiday on the French canals, Diana to make a pilgrimage to the shrine of St. James of Compostella.

"Ever since I read *The Bible in Spain* on wet Sundays, when I was a little girl, I've meant to go there. I shall persuade Mr. Digby to come with me and then I shall get the real atmosphere of Borrow."

"And I," said Jim, "shall join the expedition as a colporteur with a donkey laden with Bibles and sleeping-bags loaned from Mr. Stillwinter."

By the time they had finished their pilgrimage to Compostella it hardly seemed worth while going on to Guildford. They stayed for another hour beneath the pine trees and then returned to town, Diana dropping Jim in Bloomsbury after they had agreed that he should let her know at what time they could meet that evening to discuss future plans with Mr. Digby.

Mr. Digby arrived soon after six.

"Jim, my boy," he said, "it's a very great relief to see you again. I hardly knew what to make of your telegram and half expected to find you laid up in bed in the capable hands of your excellent Miss Griffiths. As I told you in my letter, things have gone far better than we could have hoped. I mean to say, I am afraid there is no doubt that Wake is guilty of a most dreadful crime." And he wiped his glasses in benignant satisfaction.

Diana had thought it unlikely that her father would be free to join that evening in any discussion of plans, and Jim, fearing that the house might be watched, deemed it wiser that Mr. Digby and he should avoid being seen in the neighbourhood of Warrender Street. Diana in consequence joined them in his little sitting-room in Bloomsbury soon after nine.

Mr. Digby was voted unanimously into the chair. He began by making a long and detailed statement of the events of the past fortnight and more particularly of his discoveries at Gaunt Lodge. The case against Wake appeared to be overwhelming; one detail after another confirmed the theory that he it was who had shot Petch. Jim, too, was able to furnish yet another link in the chain. When he played croquet with Wake, Wake had lent him a pair of his shoes. They fitted exactly, and, what was more, Mr. Digby was able to show that their measurement corresponded in size to the imprint left on the moor. Whether it was murder or manslaughter was a matter of less importance. If the police were put in possession of the information they held, he would have to stand his trial. He had just finished his summing up, when a message came that Miss Conyers was wanted on the telephone.

"It was from father at the House," she said on her return.

"He has just received a second anonymous letter. It's a twenty-four-hour ultimatum this time, and he says if he can help in any way, he can see either Mr. Digby or Dr. Pickering at the House at eleven."

"Good," said Mr. Digby. "To-morrow is the day. Our task is simple and straightforward. Your private sleuth, Miss Conyers, can, I suppose, be depended on to find out if Wake is still sleeping at Cornelian Lodge. I propose to call on him early next morning, after getting a note from Sir Richard empowering me to take what steps are necessary to secure a certain copy of *Mr. Badman*, together with the letter contained in it. I shall then proceed to compound a felony. Wake must restore what he has stolen; if he does not, we inform the police. I will draw up to-night a statement of the evidence against him. Jim will type three copies. You can each keep one and the third can be posted to Stillwinter with instructions to open it if I do not ask for its return in three days. I shall tell Wake at the outset that it will be no use his knocking me down or cutting my throat because, unless they hear from me to the contrary in three hours, my agents will put the machinery of the law in motion."

Jim quietly nudged Diana. Mr. Digby was evidently at the top of his form and was enjoying himself immensely.

"What," asked Jim, "will happen if the letter is not at Cornelian Lodge? It may be at Shepherd's Colne or at his bankers."

"That would make no difference. I should accompany Wake to wherever he had left the letter, after sending word to you to prolong the period of grace. Now how does that appeal to you as a line of action?"

"The plan is all right," said Jim, "but I should go instead of you. You will be dealing with sharp-witted rogues, who will stop at nothing to gain their ends."

"I thought you would say that, Jimbo. He grudges me the limelight, Miss Conyers. But, seriously, I fully intend to go to Cornelian Lodge to-morrow. To begin with, Jim, you are still a cripple; at the present moment I am more active and stronger than you. But apart altogether from that, I think my very age makes me more suited to act as an intermediary. After the way they treated you, you would find it almost impossible to rid your mind of animus. This is pre-eminently an occasion where you want a shrewd, level-headed man of business. Don't you agree with me, Miss Conyers?"

Diana smiled.

"I believe you are right, Mr. Digby," she said, "but you must promise to take care of yourself and to do nothing rash."

"And now that that is settled," the old man went on, "there remains little else for us to do. I propose that Jim goes down to the House to get from Sir Richard the few lines of written authorisation for me to act on his behalf. Don't tell him what I propose to do. It will be far better for him to remain in ignorance. As to the note, there need be nothing compromising in that, though I think reference should be made to *Mr. Badman* and the donor's letter. I shall destroy the note as soon as Wake has seen it and been convinced of my *bona fides*. In the meantime I shall draw out my report, which Jim will type on his return. Miss Conyers, we have already kept you too long. I am told that young ladies nowadays seldom retire to rest before midnight; but take an old man's advice. Have a bowl of hot bread and milk as soon as you get home and go straight to bed. It has been an exciting day for all of us."

"And one other thing," he added, as he said good night. "If I am successful to-morrow, as I have every reason to be, I should like you both to celebrate the event with me in a little dinner-party at Richmond or Kew. I know you won't refuse an old bachelor."

"Indeed I won't, Mr. Digby," and much to that gentleman's surprise, and before he knew what had happened, she had kissed him on the cheek.

XX
The Split Infinitive

THE MEETING WITH WAKE DID NOT TAKE PLACE UNTIL
the next afternoon. Mr. Digby had called in the morning at
Cornelian Lodge only to find that he was out. An elderly
man-servant informed him that Mr. Wake would be in for
lunch, and with him Mr. Digby left a message that he would
call on a matter of urgent business at two o'clock.

It was with difficulty that he persuaded Jim that there
was no need to accompany him. The interview, as he saw
it, was a straightforward matter of business, unpleasant, but
nothing more. Ample precautions had been taken against
the possibility of foul play. He wanted no unnecessary fuss.

Cornelian Lodge was a large semi-detached villa in an
altogether respectable and uninteresting suburban street.
The respectable and uninteresting man-servant informed
him that Mr. Wake would see him, and ushered him into a
sitting-room on the first floor.

"Mr. Digby," said Wake, rising from a chair, "it was a real
pleasure to get your message. I don't think you've met my

friend Dr. Kemp, before. Terry, ring for coffee, there's a good fellow. What will you smoke, Mr. Digby, cigarette, cigar, or a pipe? Neither? Then you will enjoy the flavour of the coffee all the more. The nerves of taste are intimately connected with those of smell. If both are stimulated at the same time by different stimuli, there is bound to be some blurring of sensation."

"No doubt," said Mr. Digby, as he took the chair that was offered him. "I have come, Mr. Wake, on important private business. Your friend must excuse me, but—"

"Take no notice of Dr. Kemp," Wake interrupted. "We have no secrets from each other, and if I guess your mission aright, he is almost as much concerned in the matter as I am."

Mr. Digby took out a slip of paper from his waistcoat pocket. "You might just cast your eye over that," he said. "I want you to be perfectly satisfied with my credentials... May I borrow a match? Thank you."

He walked over to the fire-place and set a light to Sir Richard's note.

"An exceedingly wise precaution," commented Wake. "If all compromising letters were dealt with in a similar manner, life for many of us would be far easier. I envy you your business training. Ah! here is the coffee. We shall be free now from interruption. I ought perhaps to inform you that it is not drugged."

"I have come," said Mr. Digby, "as I think you already know, about these threatening letters which you have sent to Sir Richard Mottram and to demand the return of the copy of *Mr. Badman* and the letter which was contained in it."

"You take a very great deal for granted, Mr. Digby. Would it not be more tactful to state a hypothetical case?"

"No, the time for tact has gone by. We may as well put all our cards on the table. I think that you will find your hand by no means as strong as you suppose."

"Kemp," said Wake, "Mr. Digby will, I know, excuse the personal reference, but don't you see an extraordinary resemblance between his face and that of the knave of clubs? Excuse me, I really must not interrupt. You were saying?"

"I was saying that it is no use beating about the bush. Unless you return the incriminating documents within three hours, my agents have instructions to put into the hands of the police evidence which will lead to your arrest for the murder of the man Petch. It will be useless for you to try and detain me or to use violence. A statement of the evidence exists in triplicate. I have made all arrangements with my agents as to how they will act."

"How exceedingly awkward!" said Wake. "It looks to us, Kemp, as if Mr. Digby were engaged in a whole-hearted attempt to upset our little apple-cart. But how are we to know that this is not a gigantic piece of bluff?"

"To show that it is not," said Mr. Digby, "I will mention only three witnesses against you: the chauffeur who handed your note to Mr. Lavender, the blood-stained sleeping-bag found buried in the rock garden, and finally the man who saw you leave Gaunt Lodge between twelve and one o'clock with the bag on your back."

Wake poured himself out a second cup of coffee. Mr. Digby thought that his face had grown paler, but his hand never shook.

"The trick," he said, "I suppose, is yours, but not, I think, the rubber. I confess that you have taken me by surprise, and with your permission I should like to have a few minutes to talk the matter over with Dr. Kemp."

The request was one which Mr. Digby did not feel he could refuse. Their plans had collapsed at the very moment when it seemed that they were to be crowned with success. Neither of the two men was a fool. Deliberation would only convince them of the fact that he held the master cards. Wake and Kemp withdrew to a distant corner of the room and with their backs towards him engaged in a whispered conversation.

"My friend and I are agreed," said Wake at last. "I speak for him as well as for myself. But before coming to the main issue, there are one or two things which I should like to clear up. Do you recognise the gentleman on the farther side of the road, who is intently admiring Dr. Kemp's begonias?"

Mr. Digby looked out of the window.

"No," he said, "I have never seen the man before. He is a complete stranger to me."

"Good," Wake went on. "He is a private inquiry agent, who has been dogging my footsteps for the last few days. He took up his station there about five minutes after you had entered the house. I very much dislike being followed. Now, supposing I hand you over what you want, what guarantee have I that this sleuth will not go at once to the police?"

"He is acting under orders, and presumably is only here to watch over my safety. But, as I told you before, he is a stranger to me."

"Then may I take it on your word of honour as a gentleman that once the book and letter are handed over to you, there will be no criminal proceedings initiated by you and your friends, and that we shall be free from the inquisitive interference of the connoisseur in begonias? I should like to point out to you—and I think you are a little in danger of forgetting it—that my position is not quite as weak as you suppose. Granted that the police take action, they have still to make out a case which depends almost entirely on circumstantial evidence. You have accepted too readily the theory of murder. There is such a thing as justifiable homicide. I might point out, too, that I am something more than a mere nobody. Can you really picture a stolid British jury connecting one of the foremost exponents of the bloodless science of economics with murder? The purport of all this is to show you that it is not so much a matter of your dictating terms as our coming to a mutual understanding."

"There is something in what you say," said Mr. Digby. "I am quite willing to give you some sort of written guarantee that you will be safe from molestation."

"In that case," said Wake, "I will get the book."

He walked over to a tall bookcase, removed a volume from one of the middle shelves, and from the space at the back took out the little book which Mr. Digby remembered so well.

"I brought it from the safe-deposit yesterday," he said. "And now about our guarantee. You will find pen and paper on the table. I'll dictate the few words that are necessary, and then if you agree to them, you can add your signature."

Mr. Digby drew a chair to the table and unscrewed the top of his fountain-pen.

"Something like this will do," said Wake.

> *"'As soon as I have received the copy of Mr. Badman and the accompanying letter, I undertake to stop at once all proceedings against Wake and Co.'"*

Mr. Digby wrote the words in his characteristically bold hand.

"Will that meet the case, Kemp?" asked Wake, as he handed him the sheet of paper.

"In all essentials, yes," said the doctor, "but I think that I should be mentioned by name. I suggest the following form of words:

> *"'When the copy of Mr. Badman and the accompanying letter are received, I undertake to immediately stop all proceedings against Wake and Kemp.'"*

"Kindly repeat the words again more slowly," said Mr. Digby. "There," he added, as he appended his signature. "I think that ought to give you what you want. The split infinitive is Dr. Kemp's. I wash my hands of it."

Kemp was standing behind his chair. Suddenly, before he realised what was happening, Mr. Digby found himself gagged and his arms firmly seized.

"Doctors," said Wake, with a smile, "are often unduly sensitive when attention is drawn to minor deficiencies in grammar. There are, however, occasions when even a split infinitive is justified."

XXI
Iron Hand in Velvet Glove

"Ring the bell for Lockwood," said Kemp, "and ask him to bring me all the silk scarves he can find and the cords from our dressing-gowns. Don't struggle, Mr. Digby. I don't want to inconvenience you more than I can help. You are a genuine old sportsman, the type of uncle I have looked for all my life and who, I had begun to fear, was non-existent. It will be necessary to detain you for a few hours, but that is all."

Mr. Digby accepted the inevitable. His legs and arms were quickly bound to the chair. When Kemp had finished, he could only glare at his captors in outraged indignation.

"Now, Mr. Digby," said Wake, "you will be able to see that occasionally a split infinitive has its uses. Lockwood, bring Mr. Digby's hat and coat and umbrella."

He went over to the table and took up the second of the two sheets of paper on which Mr. Digby had written his guarantee against police interference.

"We must make do as well as we can with this," he said, and, taking up a ruler, ran a faint pencil-line across the page.

"And now, Terry, your scissors for one minute. It would have been impossible to do this with your first draft, Mr. Digby, but by good luck your second one can be cut in two in such a way that it makes excellent sense, though not quite the sort of sense you intended. For our next proceeding we rely entirely upon your powers of observation and your assurance that you have never seen the begonia specialist before.

"Come over here, Lockwood. I want you to try on Mr. Digby's hat. Just a little large, but a slip of paper in the lining will remedy that. The coat is a quite passable fit. You keep so many things in your pockets, Mr. Digby, that your clothes tend to lose their distinctive cut. Now the spectacles and umbrella. Will he pass, Terry, do you think, presuming that our begonia expert takes no interest in the annual illustrated reports of the British and Colonial Bible Society and at the most has only studied our friend's back?

"Tuck the umbrella under your arm, Lockwood, and don't stand there like a wooden effigy. Register active benevolence, you fool, and listen carefully to what I have to say. You are to leave the house, walk down the road, and take the first bus that comes. It doesn't matter where you go to, but you must be back here in an hour. Somewhere outside the garden gate you will meet a gentleman in a bowler hat—you can see him now from the window. Ask him if he is acting under the instructions of Dr. Pickering or Miss Conyers, explaining that you are Mr. Digby. You will then hand him this note, which he is at liberty to read, with the request that he will take it to Dr. Pickering or to Miss Conyers, to whom you will telephone in the course of an hour.

"The point is, Lockwood, that for the time being you are

to impersonate Mr. Digby, who is only known by description to the inquiry agent who has been watching the house. We wish to detain Mr. Digby for a short time without suspicion being aroused. The part you have to play for a man of your varied experience of life is comparatively simple. My only trouble is that mask-like face of yours. How can we make him more benevolent, Terry?

"Don't think of your past, Lockwood, or of the wrongs of society. Try to believe that all is for the best in the best of all possible worlds. Imagine that you are a wealthy manufacturer of blankets, surrounded by a shivering populace. Picture yourself as a sturdy pillar of Liberalism. Concentrate on the nature of the Nonconformist conscience, when its awkward angles have been softened by years of easy living. And, above all, ooze benevolence. It's no good looking at Mr. Digby now. He is in the grip of passion; he is not his true self. It is the Uncle Athelstan of yesterday that we must try to realise, the kindly, quixotic old bachelor, with a finger in everyone else's pie. You see the sort of character I mean? If you see a dirty little child in the road outside, pat it on the head and give it a penny to buy sweets. That's the sort of atmosphere we want."

Lockwood gave a villainous leer, and Wake groaned.

"It's all right," said Kemp; "you can trust Lockwood not to let us down. But it's time he was off."

From his chair Mr. Digby watched Wake and Kemp, who stood in the recess by the window. He was completely ignored; all their attention was fixed on the figure of the man who was impersonating him.

"He's really not half bad," said Wake. "He's buttonholing

the man now. I think he's pulled it off, Terry. Now let's get the old boy safely fixed up."

Mr. Digby, his hands firmly tied, was led upstairs to a room at the back of the house.

"I'm going down for a glass of water," said Kemp. "I'm afraid it will be necessary to keep you gagged, but you shall have a drink first."

"Kemp is a kind-hearted fellow," Wake began, as soon as the other had gone. "I think it quite possible, if you had been his uncle, that he might have become a medical missionary. You could have allowed him a rebate on Bibles, and on blankets, too, if he avoided the tropics. Greenland's icy mountains: Business and religion walking hand in hand. But there is no use sighing over the past when the future is ours, and here comes Terry with a drink. I am glad to see that he has remembered the fact that you are a teetotaller."

The gag was removed. Mr. Digby drained the glass that was held to his lips.

"You shall suffer for this outrage, Mr. Wake," he gasped.

"Quite possibly. I am the first to admit that we are taking risks. It is illegal for us to detain you here against your will. It is equally illegal for you to propose to compound a felony. For the time being we are what Mr. Kipling has termed the lesser breeds without the law. But we wish you no harm, Mr. Digby. Your dignity will be the only thing to suffer."

The gag was replaced, his ankles and knees firmly tied together. The two men then lifted him on to the bed, Kemp placing a pillow underneath his head.

"I am afraid you are bound to be uncomfortable," he said,

"but some food and drink will be brought you in a couple of hours. It's all part of the fortunes of war, Mr. Digby."

He was left alone. The room was an attic bedroom, lit by a window high up in the wall. In one corner was an iron wash-stand, in another a wardrobe of painted deal. A couple of chairs, a chest of drawers, and the bed on which he lay completed the furniture. He closed his eyes and tried to compose his outraged feelings. He was full of malice, hate, and all uncharitableness, and what was almost worse, he had fallen below the high standard of common sense which was expected in an ordinary Bradborough business man. In mind and body he felt very sore.

But Mr. Digby was not beaten. He might be getting on in years; he might, as Wake had put it, ooze benevolence; but he would outwit them yet. He gave careful attention to the cords which secured his hands and feet. It soon, however, became obvious to him that they really did secure them. Then they would have to be cut. For long Mr. Digby pondered over the problem. At last his eyes lit up with sudden satisfaction. He sat up in bed and then, sliding down on to the floor, crawled along to where one of the chairs was standing. Then, returning to the wash-stand, he managed to pull a coarse towel from the hand-rail and to wrap it loosely round his hands.

The next step was more difficult; he had to mount a chair, whose centre of gravity seemed anything but equal to the occasion. Twice he fell, but at last he stood erect, his hands tied together over his head, wrapped in their protecting towel. He struck the window with all the force of which he was capable; there was a crash of broken glass, and in all sides of the window-frame the sharp knife-like edges which would do his work. He paused for a minute to see if he had given the alarm. No, the house was quiet. Balancing himself precariously on the chair with his hands above his head, Mr. Digby began his task. It was not easy, but the fragments of glass, fixed firmly in the putty of the window-frame, little by little cut through one strand after another of the cord which bound his wrists.

At last his hands, though bleeding, were free. The rest was a matter only of a few minutes. With a sigh of relief he mopped his streaming brow and, throwing himself down upon the bed, turned his mind to the problem of the locked door. It was half-past three, and from what Kemp had said he might expect a visitor at five with food and drink. If the broken glass outside were discovered, the visitor would almost certainly come before.

Mr. Digby was emphatically a man of peace. He advocated drastic reductions on naval and military expenditure. He was not ashamed of being called a little Englander, but he was no pacifist. The present occasion was pre-eminently one that called, if not for the knuckle-duster, at least for the iron hand in the velvet glove; and in the fender he noticed a serviceable-looking poker, that might well be adapted for his purpose.

He took it up, weighing it carefully in his hand. A horrible thing, he thought, to bring down in righteous anger on the head of the first person who entered the room. It might be Kemp, and Mr. Digby's heart was not wholly hardened against Kemp. He had placed that pillow beneath his head, as if he had really wished to make him comfortable. No, he felt that he could not conscientiously break open Kemp's head with a poker, though he could stun him with pleasure. His weapon would have to be modified. There was an old and dilapidated sponge-bag hanging on the towel-rail. Mr. Digby took it down, slit up one corner of the pillow and, after taking out a couple of handfuls of feathers, proceeded to stuff them into the bag. Into its centre he thrust the heavy knob of the poker and over all tied the two silk handkerchiefs that had bound his ankles. When he had completed his task, he felt that he was in possession of a weapon which, if a muscular Christian ought not to use, he might at least be forgiven for using.

Slowly the minutes dragged by. It was after four o'clock when at last he heard steps on the stairs. Mr. Digby took his station by the door, his hand firmly grasping the poker. He tried to banish all thoughts of pity by thinking of the intolerable insults that had been offered him, particularly of Wake's gibes.

"Oozing benevolence," he muttered, "oozing benevolence! Pat him on the head and give him a penny!" and the light of battle came into his eyes.

The steps stopped on the landing; the key turned in the lock; the door opened; and there was a heavy crash.

Mr. Digby knelt over the unconscious form of Lockwood.

"Violence is a terrible thing," he said, "but, thank God, I padded the poker."

Then, closing the door softly behind him, he crept silently downstairs.

XXII
The Blue Two-Seater

WHEN MR. DIGBY HAD FOUND HIMSELF A PRISONER IN the attic, his only thought had been how quickly he could escape from Cornelian Lodge, but as he made his way downstairs elated by the complete success of his knock-out blow, he suddenly decided to take the offensive. He had seen the letter and the book lying on the table in the sitting-room. He determined that he would not leave them there without at least one effort to get hold of them. Fortune was once again to favour him. The two doors opening on to the first-floor landing were both ajar. From the room on the right, which he had not entered, came the sound of voices. He paused for a moment outside the door. Wake was telephoning, and Kemp interposing an occasional remark. The road was clear. He entered the sitting-room on tiptoe. There on the table were the book and letter lying where Wake had left them. Hurriedly he slipped them into his pocket.

Wake was still telephoning as he passed down the stairs into the hall. From the hat-stand he took his hat, coat, and umbrella. The front door closed behind him without a sound; ten seconds later the garden gate clicked and he was out in the road. Without stopping to look back he began to run, nor did he pause for breath until he found himself on the bus route.

Forty minutes later he was back again in Bloomsbury.

To his disappointment he found that Jim was out. Miss Conyers had called in the car about four, and the two, so Miss Griffiths informed him, had left together. But there was a note for Mr. Digby which she had forgotten.

Mr. Digby retired to his room and from the recesses of his suit-case extracted the reserve pair of glasses, steel rimmed, which he invariably carried in case of emergency.

"Diana has just told me of your splendid news," he read. *"She wished that you yourself had been able to telephone, but she's keeping her thanks until this evening. We can't make out why you should have chosen the 'Golden Lion' at Chalfont St. James as our place of meeting, but we shall be there at half-past seven in accordance with your instructions. I suppose you will probably motor there direct, but I write these few lines on the off chance of your looking in at Miss Griffiths' first. I will see about the champagne."*

Mr. Digby frowned, and re-read the letter. Chalfont St. James! He knew nothing of the place except that it was somewhere in Buckinghamshire. The message came, of course, from Wake, but what could it mean? Surely they could gain nothing by an attempt to kidnap Diana?

He rang the bell for Miss Griffiths.

"I want you to telephone to the nearest garage," he said, "and ask them to send their fastest car round here at once. And as soon as you have done that bring me two eggs, lightly boiled, some tea and bread and butter. Be as quick as you can, Miss Griffiths, please, the matter is urgent."

By the time he had changed and sat down to a hurried meal it was nearly half-past five. If Wake for some reason wanted Diana at Chalfont St. James, then Diana must be stopped. That was his problem in a nutshell, but the nut was hard to crack. Mr. Digby broke open the skull of his second egg and wondered how that poor man Lockwood was feeling. Suddenly he remembered that he was now the possessor of *Mr. Badman*. Would it be safe to leave the book and letter under lock and key in his lodgings, or ought he to burn the letter at once? Finally he decided to send both in a registered parcel to Sir Richard Mottram and to notify him by telegram of their recovery. The car arrived. He drove first to the nearest post-office and then told the man to call at the British Automobile Club.

Many years before Mr. Digby had reluctantly been persuaded to become a member. Every January he wrote out the cheque for his annual subscription with the determination that it should be his last. As far as he could see the only advantage he received was an occasional sense of moral superiority reflected from his chauffeur when the club scouts saluted him at cross-roads. He determined to put the organisation to the test. After five minutes spent in interviewing officials who passed him on from one to the other with polite indifference, he found himself at last in the presence of a young man, immaculately dressed, in an office designed to express the spirit of unruffled efficiency. Two vases filled with roses stood on the mantelpiece on either side of a statuette representing Speed, a young woman in flowing drapery perched precariously on one foot on the top of a bronze precipice.

"I want," he said, "to get a message through to a blue two-seater Morton Ashby car that left town soon after four for Chalfont St. James. It's quite likely that the car did not go there direct; it's possible that they may have stopped on the way. But it's most important that it should be stopped before it reaches Chalfont St. James. I thought possibly you might telephone through to your scouts."

"I am afraid the matter is a little outside our province," said the young man with a suppressed yawn. "Have you spoken to Mr. Machlin?"

"If Mr. Machlin is the courteous head porter, I have. If he is the man with the monocle and the white spats, I have. If he is the efficiency expert on the first floor, I have. If he is the comedian who was giggling with the typists on the second floor, I have."

"If Mr. Machlin is still about, you had better see him," said the young man. "Third door on the right down the passage. Good afternoon."

"Good afternoon," said Mr. Digby. "I shall resign at once from this Club and transfer my Annual Subscription to the Crippled Children's Benevolent Association."

Mr. Digby, however, had not exhausted his resources. He rang up a garage in Beaconsfield, explained to the proprietor what he wanted, and got him to promise to send one of his men to intercept, if possible, Diana's car and to detain it until he should have arrived on the scene. It was a quarter-past six. If Jim had gone direct to Chalfont St. James it would be too late to stop him, but Mr. Digby thought that it was possible that he might loiter on the way. He had spoken in his note of Diana and not Miss Conyers. The fact was significant, more significant indeed than the reference to champagne. If he, Mr. Digby, were in his nephew's place, he would waste no time in coming to an understanding with Miss Conyers. He hoped the boy had done the sensible and proper thing.

Driver and car were all that Mr. Digby had a right to expect, but for the first time in his life he complained of going slow. What on earth, he wondered, could be the meaning of this new move of Wake's? Was it some last desperate venture, or part of a long-thought-out scheme? And might they not after all abandon it when they discovered that the all-important letter was no longer in their possession?

Then suddenly at a cross-roads he saw a blue two-seater and two waving figures. He shouted to the driver to stop, the car was backed, and Mr. Digby, smiling a little sheepishly, got out.

"We were waylaid a quarter of an hour ago," said Jim, "by a ruffian in a side-car who demanded fifteen shillings and told us to proceed no further. I gather from the way he talked that he took us for motor thieves. What in the world has happened?"

"It's a queer story," said Mr. Digby. "I have the letter all right, but tell me first how you came to be here?"

"To begin at the beginning," said Jim, "I wasn't altogether

happy at your going off alone this afternoon, so we arranged with Davis, the inquiry agent, to keep an eye on Cornelian Lodge. Some time after three he presented himself at Warrender Street with this note which he said you had given him."

Jim pulled out from his waistcoat pocket a slip of paper which he handed to Mr. Digby.

> *"Immediately stop all proceedings against Wake and Kemp.*
>
> *"ATHELSTAN DIGBY."*

"I wrote that right enough," said Mr. Digby, "in peculiar circumstances that I will describe later. And what happened then?"

"Davis told me I was to expect a telephone message from you," said Diana. "At half-past three I was rung up by someone who gave the address of a provision shop in Hampstead, who said that you had not been able to get through but had left the message. I can't remember the actual words, but it was something like this: 'I have secured the letter. Meet me without fail in the Blue Bird at the "Golden Lion," Chalfont St. James, at 7.30 p.m. this evening.' Then I called for Jim and we came along."

"And, as I hoped, you dawdled by the way."

"Shall we tell him, Diana?" asked Jim.

"My dear," said Mr. Digby, "I think I know already. There are some forms of happiness which it is impossible to conceal. I congratulate you both from the bottom of my heart, but time presses. I must tell you briefly what has happened since last I saw you, and then hurry on to Chalfont St. James."

"Mr. Digby," said Diana when he had finished, and though she smiled, her eyes were moist with tears, "I think you are perfectly splendid. My blood boils when I think of those beasts treating you like that. However can I thank you for all that you have done?"

"Didn't I always tell you that there was no one like him?" said Jim. "The padded poker! That's uncle all over. But what on earth is their little game?"

"I am going to see," said Mr. Digby. "Diana and you had better get some dinner in Beaconsfield while I make a preliminary investigation. I had an excellent tea, with two boiled eggs, before I started."

Of course they refused, but after some discussion it was agreed that Jim should accompany Mr. Digby in his car while Diana stayed in Beaconsfield, where she could telephone to her father and explain what had happened.

It was a quarter to eight when they entered the long High Street of Chalfont St. James. At Jim's suggestion they passed the "Golden Lion" and drew up at a smaller inn, the "King's Arms," where they left the car. Few people were about; shop shutters were already going up; an old lady in a garden was busy watering her lilies. What connection had this village, preparing for its peaceful dreams, with Mr. Badman?

Mr. Digby and Jim had no plans other than to await events. The "Golden Lion" was an old-fashioned inn that seemed to have made a somewhat pitiful attempt to attract the passing motorist. The landlord promised that he would do his best to produce some cold supper and they were shown into the dining-room.

"I am afraid," said Mr. Digby, "that it will be useless to

ask for champagne. I shall drink your health in coffee, which after all is both warm and stimulating. I must say that I find this place depressing."

It was a large room. At one end a piano stood on a raised platform. A pile of jazz music littered one of the tables. A stuffed and highly varnished pike hung in a glass case above the fire-place, in which a pot of artificial chrysanthemums stood backed by a screen of mauve crinkly paper. Motor-charabancs, the local masonic lodge, an anglers' club, smoking concerts, all seemed to have left their mark on the character of the room.

But the cold beef was good, the cheese excellent.

The two men sat at a table in a recess by the window, screened in its lower half by lace curtains. They were just finishing their meal, when a car drew up outside and a man got out. Both recognised Wake.

"What are we to do now?" asked Jim.

"Possess our souls in patience," Mr. Digby replied, "and trust that he will not come in here."

Whatever Wake's purpose was, he did not stay long. He disappeared into the bar, and five minutes later came out again in conversation with the landlord. He got into his car and drove off down the London road in the direction from which he had come.

"I think," said Mr. Digby, "that a few words with our land-lord are indicated at this point. Jim, you had better ask for some cigars."

The proprietor of the "Golden Lion" was a kindly little man with a gift of talk. He hoped the gentlemen had been satisfied; if he had known of their coming half an hour before he could have promised them a really nice bit of steak. He wasn't one of those who believed in frozen meat from the Argentine. All the goodness was bound to go. You had only to remember the heat of the tropics. It was the same with Australian apples. There was nothing like home-killed, and he had yet to find the apple that could beat a good English Blenheim orange.

"I think," said Mr. Digby, "I know the gentleman who was speaking to you just now, a Mr. Olaf Wake."

"Oh indeed, sir. He seemed a pleasant-spoken gentleman, with rather peculiar notions, if I may say so, about Irish whisky. He was expecting to meet a friend here, and seemed rather put out when I told him I'd seen nothing of a blue two-seater. And the curious thing about it is that he isn't the only one who has been looking out for that car. I told him that the gentleman in the private bar had been making inquiries, but he didn't seem interested."

"As a matter of fact," said Mr. Digby, "I passed a blue two-seater on the road a couple of hours ago. My friend and I might perhaps have a word or two with the gentleman in the private bar."

"I'm sure he would be very glad to see you, sir. He's a retiring sort of gentleman and has been there for the last hour and a half by himself. It would be a kindness to give him your company."

"He isn't by any chance a middle-aged man with a red beard?" asked Mr. Digby.

"Oh no, sir, he's quite young and clean-shaven."

With a feeling of renewed confidence he made his way to the private bar followed by Jim.

XXIII
The Gentleman in the Private Bar

THE ROOM WAS SMALL AND COSY. IN AN ARM-CHAIR BY the fire-place, a glass of whisky on the round table by his side, sat a man whom neither Mr. Digby nor Jim had seen before. As the door opened he turned round with a start. It was a pale, handsome face that interrogated them with a glance in which suspicion and a certain veiled hostility lurked.

"I hope we are not intruding," said Mr. Digby. "My nephew and I heard from the landlord that you had been inquiring about a blue two-seater which you were expecting to meet here. We have just motored down from London and passed a car like the one he described a little way out of Beaconsfield."

"It looks as if my friend must have met with a breakdown," said the stranger. "I've been waiting now since half-past seven in this confounded pub. I suppose there's nothing for it but to go on waiting," and he looked at his watch impatiently.

"You don't happen by chance," Mr. Digby asked, "to

know a Mr. Olaf Wake who was making inquiries here about a similar car a quarter of an hour ago?"

The stranger turned towards him with a look of surprise.

"Wake?" he said, "no, I've never heard of the name. Is he an elderly bald-headed fellow?"

"The man I mean is the distinguished economist—tall and clean-shaven. He wears rimless glasses."

"No, I've never heard of him. Economists are not in my line. I should think his inquiries are only a matter of coincidence."

Mr. Digby and Jim had sat down, Mr. Digby opposite to the stranger, Jim in an arm-chair that was somewhat in the shadow. While the stranger was speaking he had been watching him intently. Taking a note-book from his pocket he scribbled something on a page and, tearing it out, handed it to Mr. Digby.

"Excuse me," he said, "I've just remembered that address you were asking for at supper."

Mr. Digby glanced at it with a slightly puzzled expression.

"Many thanks," he said, "I thought it was somewhere off Oxford Street. I'll try and call round there to-morrow."

The conversation began to flag. The stranger took up a paper, and slightly turned away from Mr. Digby as if hinting that he did not wish to be interrupted. Jim got up from his seat to examine a large scale map of the district that hung on the wall.

His movements seemed to annoy the other.

"Are you motoring far to-night?" he asked.

"I don't think so, but this part of Buckinghamshire is new to me, and maps are always interesting. I never knew, for example, until now that the criminal lunatic asylum at Eastmoor is only ten miles away."

He swung round sharply as he spoke and looked the man in the eyes. He was certain now that the suspicion that had haunted his mind for the last ten minutes was correct, and dimly he began to perceive a purpose in Wake's mysterious doings.

"You are Neville Monkbarns," he said.

The man got up from his chair. All the colour seemed to have left his face.

"You damned liar!" he exclaimed, "clear out of this room before I kick you out!"

But to Mr. Digby conviction, too, had come.

"Jim," he said, "perhaps you had better leave the matter to me. This gentleman denies that he is Neville Monkbarns, and he is right. Richard Mottram, I want you to believe that you have friends in whom you can trust, though for the moment they may appear to you as enemies."

The light died out of Mottram's eye.

"It's the old tale once again," he said. "I suppose every asylum doctor gets those words off by heart. They are all our friends; they are always doing the best for us, but at Eastmoor they take good care to lock us up for life. No, I can't go back. I don't know who you are, but you've got to deal with a desperate man."

"I think," said Mr. Digby, "that you will go back, and though perhaps it will be the most difficult thing you have ever done, you will go back of your own free will. I have addressed you by your own name, Richard Mottram. You have guarded your secret well, but others know it who are your father's enemies and who are prepared to use their knowledge to drag his reputation in the dirt. It is a long and complicated story, but I must try and tell you something of it so that you can judge for yourself."

"And that devil Wake is the man who was here half an hour ago," said Mottram when Mr. Digby had finished. "If I had only known. Oh, it's a pretty piece of villainy right enough! He'd ruin my father and use me as a pawn in the game, as you'll see when you've heard my version of the story.

"About a week ago I got a letter. It didn't come through the post, of course—never mind how it came, we have our own channels of communication with the outside world. This letter was typewritten. It bore no address, but it was signed Diana, and I at once concluded that it was from my step-sister. The writer said that steps would be taken in the course of the next ten days to arrange for my escape from Eastmoor. The fellow who had the job in hand was called Fletcher and I was given a pretty detailed description of him. I should think the betting is ten to one that he is the same as Lockwood. I met the man twice, and he struck me as just cut out for the job, a cool, competent, secretive sort of devil. We have a certain amount of liberty at Eastmoor, though it's not quite the sort of gilded cage that some of the papers make it out to be, and I've always got on well with the attendants. I fancy Fletcher must have managed to get round one or two of them. Anyhow, our meetings were not interrupted. I saw him for the last time on Saturday, when he gave me full details of the plan.

"We've been working at a nine-hole golf course in the

park. The arrangement was that I was to slip away and make for the boundary wall at a spot where for a hundred yards it skirts the Ockshotte road. Fletcher promised that I should find a ladder at the foot of a poplar tree. I was to climb the wall and then hide the ladder. A quarter of a mile farther down the lane, behind a hay stack, Fletcher was to plant a bicycle and a suit-case so that I could change my clothes. Then the idea was that I should push on slowly across country to Chalfont St. James, feed at the 'Golden Lion,' and wait there until a blue two-seater called for me somewhere about half-past seven."

"So that was Wake's plan," said Mr. Digby. "No wonder he felt pleased with himself this morning. With that letter of yours and all the information he possessed I think he could have ruined Sir Richard. But this would have clinched the matter. Miss Conyers would have arrived here in a car that plenty of witnesses would have been prepared to swear to. For Wake's purpose it would not matter if she actually saw you or not. As soon as her car arrived at the 'Golden Lion' he would get in touch with the police. At the time she could easily explain her presence. She might even deny all knowledge of you if the question were asked her, though somehow I do not think she would do that. The real significance of her presence would be revealed later. I can picture how Wake would set to work. Queer rumours would go the round of the clubs. Then some rag of a Sunday paper would begin hinting things."

"What sort of communications passed between you and Lockwood?" asked Jim. "I suppose you burned his letters?"

"Yes," said Mottram, "I took good care to do that. The

only note I wrote to him was on Sunday, addressed to him under an alias at a Hampstead branch post-office. We agreed on the words 'All right for Monday' if everything seemed in order at my end, and at his suggestion I signed it 'Dick.' I remember at the time being rather amused at what I thought was only a coincidence. But that reminds me. In one of the inside pockets of the suit I'm wearing, the suit you know that the loving forethought of Wake provided for me, I found this letter. It's typewritten as you can see."

"Dear Dick," read Mr. Digby, "I write these few lines to tell you to keep a good heart and that I shall be with you a few hours after you get this.

"DIANA."

"I was really rather touched," Mottram went on, as he lit a match and set fire to the paper. "I had made up my mind that I should never see or hear from her or my father again. And then in these last ten days it looked as if I had been mistaken, that they had not forgotten me after all. Well, I suppose it's understandable enough. I'm a murderer, and that makes all the difference unless you happen to be an asylum attendant. After a time they do regard you as a human being. But after all, what does it matter if I don't owe my freedom to my sister? I still am free. I have money in my pocket, and you, sir, could lend me a fiver to help to tide over things. What has Wake got to do with it?"

Mr. Digby looked at his watch; it was nearly nine o'clock.

"Jim," he said, "I'm not quite easy about Miss Conyers.

That tell-tale car of hers is too near to Chalfont St. James. I think you ought to get her back to town. Get our chauffeur to run you over to Beaconsfield. He can come back for me at the 'King's Arms,' when I've had some further talk with Mr. Mottram."

Jim himself was beginning to be anxious about Diana.

"Very well," he said. "Good-night, Mottram. You can trust my uncle to do the right thing."

Mr. Digby was silent for some minutes after he had left.

"Without prejudice to your future actions," he said at last, "I think we had better get away from this place. Wake may turn up at any moment. He may already have put the police on your tracks. We will walk along the road in the direction in which you came. That is where they will least expect to find you. We shall be able to talk undisturbed."

XXIV
The Last Encounter

Dusk had already fallen when the two men left the "Golden Lion." They walked down the High Street and took the turning to the right, by the church. It was a narrow lane bounded by cherry orchards and market gardens.

"When I was a young man," said Mr. Digby, "I had serious thoughts of becoming a painter. I would have given anything to escape from the family business. I saw no scope for the artistic temperament in the manufacture of blankets."

"I should have thought you would have had the courage of your convictions," said Mottram.

"As a matter of fact I had. My convictions were different from my inclinations. I was never intimate with my father, but he was a man whom I respected. He was getting old, losing his business grip, and his two partners were fools. I was young and energetic, and though I disliked the work, I had plenty of self-confidence. Then I had an only sister, an invalid, who would have lost what little happiness she got from life if I had gone to London or Paris. So I stuck it out. I'm glad I did. I made a success of business, where as an artist I should have failed. I know enough, though, to appreciate the work of others and to realise the difficulties that they have been able to surmount."

"And the moral of all this!" asked Mottram.

"It's not part of the artist's business to point a moral," said Mr. Digby with a smile. "I'm not suggesting for a minute that there is any parallel between my desire to escape from business and your desire to be free. But we both had a father and a sister to consider. If the firm had gone under, the old man's heart would have been broken. If you make good your escape, Mottram, there is no telling how much of your past may escape with you. If I lent you money, what would you do when that money was exhausted? You say you would find work. I believe you would look for it; I am convinced you would not find it.

"A young fellow came to me the other day. He had taken an honours degree in chemistry; he was trained in business methods; his character was excellent; he had held a research fellowship for a year; and for the last three months he had been earning his keep by helping his landlord with a milk round. You have had your chance, one that many men would have jumped at, and you have failed. You speak of going free, but in a month or two you would be the slave of your environment, a drug-driven automaton. I don't want to be harder than I ought, but if you in some measure have been a victim of circumstance, others have been your victims."

"She was more of a devil than a woman," said Mottram, huskily, "and at least I loved her."

"And Petch's daughter, and poor Petch himself?" asked

Mr. Digby. "No, Mottram, it seems to me that even if escape were justifiable, the time for it is not now."

Mottram was silent for some minutes.

"Safer locked up," he said at last. "That's about what it comes to. Well, I suppose you are right, Mr. Digby. I'll go back, but you had better see me a little farther on my way. Second thoughts are not always best."

Mr. Digby put his arm in his.

"I don't see very well at night," he said, "especially with these glasses, which are not the ones I usually wear. You are acting as a gentleman and as a man of honour."

Mottram laughed.

"That's something new at least," he said. "But if I am going back I may as well do the thing properly. My own clothes ought to be in that suit-case underneath the hay stack. I'll go round that way, change, and scale the wall. Then when I finally present myself to the authorities I'll spin a yarn of having fallen asleep in the park. They won't believe me, but they won't be able to prove that I've tried to escape, and the matter will soon blow over. It will make things easier, too, for the fellows there whom Lockwood squared. I don't want to get them into a row."

They had reached a spot where the road took a sudden bend. On turning the corner they saw a motor-cycle and side-car drawn up by the side of the hedge. The driver apparently was engaged upon some repairs. He looked up as they passed and then bent down over the machinery.

"Good-night," he said, "the road's clear."

Mottram laughed.

"It's all right, Simmons," he said, "the game's up. I'm going back home like a good boy, and you may as well give me a lift. This is my friend, Mr. Digby, who has put me wise about one or two little things. Simmons was one of the good fellows I was telling you about whom I feared might get into hot water."

"Oh! I can look after myself all right," said Simmons. "I'm out looking for you now, and you can take it from me that I haven't seen you, unless you've really changed your mind."

"Well you see I have. I thought my friends were planning this get-away, but it seems that I'm mistaken. It was a fellow called Wake, whom I'd never heard of, but who wanted to get me and my pals into hot water. So it's back to the army again, sergeant."

"Well, I'm jiggered," said the other. "It looks to me as if your Mr. Wake deserves to get it in the neck from someone. He had better not show up in this neighbourhood, that's all. Tampering with a man's honesty and all to no purpose."

Mr. Digby's hand had gone to his pocket.

"Mr. Simmons," he said, taking out a five-pound note, "I don't believe in tampering with a man's honesty, but as a justice of the peace I like to be able at times to acknowledge a kind action. You have played the game. Mr. Monkbarns is returning with you of his own free will. I have been discussing the matter with him and we agree that there is no reason why it should be ever known that he has gone beyond the bounds of Eastmoor Park. And now I think it is time I was getting back—tut-tut, man, of course you must accept it, I insist."

He shook both men by the hand.

"God bless you," he said to Mottram. "You've done the right thing."

Then before they had time to reply he had turned his back to them and walked off down the road.

"That's a fine sporting old gentleman," said Simmons. "He reminds me of my Uncle George who was manager of Wednesbury Athletic the year they got into the third round of the cup. Come along, Monkbarns, we had better be getting a move on." He swung himself into the saddle and started the engine.

"Half a minute till I get a light," said Mottram. He had just struck a match when the silence of the night was broken by a short, sharp cry.

"Quick," said Mottram, "it's old Digby," and, followed by Simmons, he ran down the road.

A hundred yards from the spot where they had left him a motor-car was standing. In the white patch of light cast by its lamps two men were struggling. Again there was a cry, and the shorter of the two fell. But Mottram had already thrown himself upon the assailant. He saw a pale, spectacled face, convulsed with rage. To and fro the two men swayed. Wake was the taller and he had got the better grip. To Mottram's surprise the man knew how to wrestle. Tighter and tighter grew his grip. The face opposed to his own was no longer pale, but livid. Then Wake tripped over the prostrate form of Mr. Digby. Quick as lightning Mottram seized his advantage. The man fell beneath him, his head striking the corner of the footboard of the car.

"That's the blighter who would have double-crossed us," said Mottram, as he picked himself up.

"How is Mr. Digby? Dirty work at the cross-roads to-night, Simmons, I'm afraid."

They bent over the old man's prostrate form while

Simmons, who had knowledge in such matters, examined his limbs.

"There are no bones broken," he said at last. "Good, he's opening his eyes. How do you feel, Mr. Digby, now? Not so bad? Don't be in a hurry to get up, sir."

"Where's Wake?" he murmured. "Where's Wake? I'm all right."

"Wake's unconscious and quite comfortable. Don't you worry about him."

In a minute or two Mr. Digby was sitting up.

"I'm really very much obliged to you both," he said. "The man was passing in his car and set on me almost without warning. What are we to do with him?"

Simmons went over to where Wake was lying.

"I should think he's got concussion," he said. "It won't hurt him to lie in a dry ditch for a bit. We'll run the car off the road and make it look like an accident."

"And then," said Mottram, "you had better take Mr. Digby back to Chalfont St. James in your side-car; you can report the matter there and pick me up later. His car was to call for him at the 'King's Head.'"

Mr. Digby, bruised and badly shaken, was helped into the side-car, and ten minutes later Simmons had transferred his charge to the chauffeur with an injunction to drive carefully as the old gentleman had met with an accident.

"I shall be all right," said Mr. Digby, as he gave the address in Bloomsbury.

But when soon after midnight the car drew up in Coram Road, it was a limp, unconscious form that Jim and the chauffeur lifted tenderly and carried into the house.

XXV
At Deepdale End

IT WAS HALF-PAST THREE. MR. DIGBY HAD HAD HIS afternoon sleep and was lying in his *chaise longue* in the orchard, his books and papers on a table by his side. The whir of the mowing machine, drowsy, monotonous, came up to him from the lawn, where Johnson the gardener, with the aid of the reluctant Samuel Albert, was hard at work preparing the court for to-morrow's tennis. In between the softly swaying apple boughs he could see the purpling moors. The heather would not be at its best, Diana had said, until the end of the month, but already it was flecked with the gold of the turning bracken.

Mr. Digby took a silk handkerchief from his pocket and carefully polished his glasses. His face without them looked old and worn, but once their bridge had fallen into the deep groove that furrowed his nose, his eyes lit up with their old vivacity. The owner of the house was back again in his study looking out of the windows, watching the little maid making her way towards him through the long grass of the orchard.

There was no afternoon delivery, but one of the keepers had been into Keldstone and had called at the post-office. There were two letters for Mr. Digby and a registered parcel.

"Is there anything I can get for you, sir?" asked the maid.

"You might raise the back of my chair a little. That's better." He was quite comfortable, but the girl was always being put in her place by the housekeeper, and he knew that she liked to wait on him. He took his scissors from his pocket and cut the string of the parcel. It contained a letter and a book. He recognised the writing of Sir Richard Mottram; the book, too, he had seen before, though the binding was new.

"Dear Mr. Digby," he read,

"I hope that by the time this reaches you the rest and quiet of Deepdale End will have set you on the high road of complete recovery. When we talked together ten days ago I tried very inadequately to express our thanks for all that you have done. It is a debt that can never be repaid, but I know of no one to whom I would rather be indebted than yourself. It is a pleasure to think that in the years to come we shall see more and more of each other, and if I wanted any further assurance of Diana's future happiness—and I do not— it would be in the knowledge that Pickering is your nephew. You will be interested in further news of Mr. Badman (by the way, I have had the old copy rebound; I thought you might like to keep it; it is yours by right of purchase and every other right). Wake, as you know, was treated for concussion, in the hospital at High Wycombe. I understand that he is now convalescent.

His injuries were put down to a motor accident and he seems content to leave it at that. I think it quite probable that he did not recognise Dick, but thought that he and Simmons were ordinary travellers who could witness to his having assaulted you. I imagine that he was scouring the roads in a vain attempt to find the Blue Bird, and that when he met you unexpectedly the sight of the man who had continuously thwarted his deep-laid schemes was too much for him. I don't know if you saw a paragraph in yesterday's Times announcing that he had reconsidered a pressing invitation to accept a new Chair of International Relations at an American University. 'No one,' it was said, 'could be better qualified.' I suppose we must put no obstacle in the way of his getting his passport, and that once again Ellis Island will detain the wrong people. An intimate friend of mine in the city has furnished me with some illuminating particulars about his financial transactions in which you will be interested. I enclose his letter.

"I must thank you for your very kind congratulations, all the more welcome when I realise that we are political opponents. The direction of our foreign policy at this juncture is a very grave responsibility. I go to my task with a mind freed from an intolerable incubus, with the strenuous endeavour to do my best not only for this country but for the peace of Europe. With all good wishes for a speedy recovery, in which Lady Mottram joins.

"Yours very sincerely,
"RICHARD MOTTRAM.

"P.S.—I was speaking to the Prime Minister the other day about the Royal Commission it is proposed to set up, dealing with the export from this country of historic works of art. I ventured to suggest your name as one who is in close touch with our provincial galleries. He at once agreed—had heard of you from Phelps and Sir Halliday Arbuthnot. I hope you will consent to serve."

Mr. Digby was enormously pleased. For the moment he forgot all about Wake in the honour done him. Fancy Sir Halliday Arbuthnot remembering him! He had only seen the great man on three occasions. It was really very gratifying. He took off his spectacles and repolished them with vigour. Then he turned to Sir Richard Mottram's enclosure.

"It is curious that you should have been asking about Olaf Wake," he read, "as I have been a good deal interested in that gentleman's financial dealings of late years. He is a man of altogether extraordinary ability, the economic theorist who puts his knowledge to practical use and incidentally succeeds in feathering his own nest. I first met him after the war. He had an almost uncanny flair for predicting the unpredictable in the fluctuation of exchanges and must have netted a small fortune. I believe that he was entrusted with the management of some Irish Political Fund. Anyhow, he had a free hand and made the most of it. But he was badly hit at the time of your appointment. I think he must have been banking on Ellis Hanbury going to

the F.O. and for a continuation of the old policy with Russia, though if anyone asked his opinion he always maintained that a break was coming. I found out the other day that he had been secretly investing in Polish securities. At the price he paid for them he would have stood to gain enormously if the old regime had contin-ued. As it is with everything again in the melting-pot he must have lost very heavily indeed. It was a pure gamble. There were the Siberian mining concessions too. The negotiations were practically completed, and now I suppose everything will have to start from the beginning again. Wake is not the only man in the city who has reason to regret that you ever left the Home Office. For goodness sake, old man, go slow."

"I am inclined to agree with the writer," said Mr. Digby to himself. "If some of these political hot-heads had been in the blanket business, they would have kept cooler. But all the same it's very interesting."

He took out a pocket-book and placed the two letters in it. It was Mr. Badman's dossier. From it he extracted two other letters that he had received in the course of the week and proceeded to re-read them. The first one was signed "William Simmons" and was written in answer to a request that Mr. Digby had made to him when they parted at the "King's Head."

"The young gentleman arrived back safely on Tuesday night," he read, "and got no chill through sleeping out in the Park, though he has had to keep to the house

since. I will do my best to find something to interest him. He fancies scenario writing for the films, so if you will send along some books I'll do my best to see that he gets them. The talent's there all right and he has some of the best material here to draw upon which it's a cruel shame should go to waste. As I tell him, many a film writer would give a lot to be in his shoes. About books, he asked me to say that there's quite a good library, but mostly history, biography, travel and standard fiction. He would like to get hold of that new history of the Grand National. If you sent the book to me I would see that he got it."

Mr. Digby had already made inquiries for the volume, but not of his Bradborough bookseller, who was an agent for the Society for the Propagation of Christian Knowledge. The second letter that he re-read was from Terry Kemp. It was written from Cornelian Lodge.

"Just a line," he read, "of genuine condolence on your accident. I think you will believe me when I say that I had nothing whatever to do with it and deeply regret the inability to rise above petty questions of personal rancour displayed on that occasion. Your muffled poker was an admirable example of the way in which life's difficulties should be met. Lockwood's skull was fractured, but the fracture was not depressed, though for a fortnight the man himself has been. It was an unexpected blow to him, but he has learnt the necessity of not under-estimating an opponent and will in future

be suspicious of all forms of active benevolence. I am a rolling stone, Mr. Digby, but a gentleman adventurer like yourself. I am just off on a bootlegging expedition to the West Indies. I shall not be taking Lockwood with me. Will you come as my guest? I can promise you plenty of excitement and the liquor is really poisonous stuff calculated to forward the cause of Temperance which I know you have so much at heart. My kind remembrances to Dr. Pickering. Though not without an adventurous spirit he lacks your irresistible abandon. Perhaps it is because he walks in the dark shadow of impending marriage. He handled the affair at York, however, in a masterly fashion. There are many ways in which I might sign this letter. Yours respectfully, yours sincerely, would both be equally true. But I should prefer to write myself as,

> *"Yours affectionately,*
> *"Terry Kemp."*

"A plausible and attractive rascal," thought Mr. Digby. "I don't like to think of him engaged in that iniquitous rum-running business." But all the same he did think of him, and it must be confessed that Mr. Digby's brow was wholly unclouded. He saw blue seas, laughing n—oes, hard-swearing sailors, screaming parrots, Captain Cuttles and Long John Silvers. The old boy sighed.

Looking up he saw Diana and Jim coming towards him through the orchard.

"Well, my dear," he said, "there is no need to ask you if you have enjoyed your walk, and you can't begin too soon to get Jim into training. He is a bit of a humbug, you know, always talking about long tramps which never come off, and making out to be a Borrow enthusiast, and never happier than when he is tinkering with a car. Some day next year I shall make an unexpected call upon you and claim him for the walking tour he owes me. I suppose you have come to tell me that tea is ready."

"It will be in a few minutes. The Stillwinters are coming and we are having it on the terrace."

"Then I will get you to give me your arm, my dear, and Jim will follow us with my paraphernalia."

They found Mr. Stillwinter in a bantering mood.

"You and I, Digby," he said, "at our time of life are bound to expect heart attacks if we plunge at a moment's notice from the quiet of a countryside like this into our abominable metropolis. He hurried away from Gaunt Lodge, Miss Conyers, as if it were the abode of malefactors, and, as you see, he did not return to it. I can only account for his actions by supposing that he proposed to Anne and was summarily rejected, and I am afraid Miss Conyers has been too busy to comfort him."

"Philip, how can you talk such nonsense!" ejaculated his sister.

"I'm ruled with such a rod of iron at home that I'm bound to break out when I visit my friends. It's a sort of off-licence which the authorities should never refuse. I make a present of the idea to Miss Conyers."

"And I," said Diana, laughing, "am entirely on Miss Stillwinter's side. We shall have our revenge," she went on. "I got this morning a book called *Pertinent Questions*. It is a series of general knowledge papers, all of which have been answered by more or less competent people, sometimes with such poor success that it is quite encouraging for ordinary folk.

"Here, for example, is paper No. 19, in which a lieutenant-colonel scores 49 and a subaltern 83 per cent. Jim, as a late captain in the R.A.M.C., ought to be somewhere in the sixties. Come, Jim, get a pencil and paper and score for us. Miss Stillwinter shall be entrusted with the answers. She is the only person who can be depended upon not to cheat."

They reluctantly agreed to the exposure of their ignorance. Mr. Digby had no knowledge of what first-aid should be given to a person suffering from an epileptic fit, but he scored full marks over the two famous painters whose fathers were millers. He also knew what Jason went in search of, because, as he explained, a golden fleece was the trade-mark of his blankets.

Mr. Stillwinter was very indignant at the official location of Ararat. Having been there himself he insisted that he ought to know, and he preferred ignorance to knowledge when asked to state what he knew of Ramon Novarro. At the last question but one he and Mr. Digby had both scored 75, which, as Jim pointed out, indicated a mental calibre equivalent to that of a sergeant-major.

"Now Digby," said Stillwinter, excitedly, "this for the hole. Who wrote the *Life and Death of Mr. Badman*? He doesn't know, Miss Conyers; you've only to look at him to see he doesn't know. Confess, Digby, that you were about to say Daniel Defoe?"

Mr. Digby shook his head. "I give it up," he said with a smile "Was it Fielding?"

"John Bunyan, my boy. I go up top and I'll ask you another. What was the March of the Blanketeers? You don't know that. My friend Olaf Wake should be here. He would be the man to score at this game."

Again Mr. Digby smiled.

If you've enjoyed *The Mysterious Mr. Badman*,
you won't want to miss

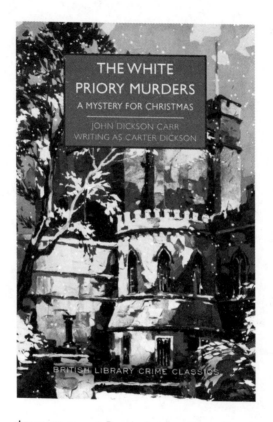

the most recent BRITISH LIBRARY CRIME CLASSIC
published by Poisoned Pen Press,
an imprint of Sourcebooks.

Don't miss these favorite British Library Crime Classics available from Poisoned Pen Press!

Mysteries written during the Golden Age of Detective Fiction, beloved by readers and reviewers

Praise for the
British Library Crime Classics

"Carr is at the top of his game in this taut whodunit... The British Library Crime Classics series has unearthed another worthy golden age puzzle."

—*Publishers Weekly*, STARRED Review,
for *The Lost Gallows*

"A wonderful rediscovery."

—*Booklist*, STARRED Review, for *The Sussex Downs Murder*

"First-rate mystery and an engrossing view into a vanished world."

—*Booklist*, STARRED Review, for *Death of an Airman*

"A cunningly concocted locked-room mystery, a staple of Golden Age detective fiction."

—*Booklist*, STARRED Review, for *Murder of a Lady*

"The book is both utterly of its time and utterly ahead of it."

—*New York Times Book Review* for *The Notting Hill Mystery*

"As with the best of such compilations, readers of classic mysteries will relish discovering unfamiliar authors, along with old favorites such as Arthur Conan Doyle and G.K. Chesterton."

—*Publishers Weekly*, STARRED Review, for *Continental Crimes*

"In this imaginative anthology, Edwards—president of Britain's Detection Club—has gathered together overlooked criminous gems."

—*Washington Post* for *Crimson Snow*